Mills & Boon
Best Seller Romance

A chance to read and collect some of the best-loved novels
from Mills & Boon—the world's largest publisher of
romantic fiction.

Every month, four titles by favourite Mills & Boon authors
will be re-published in the *Best Seller Romance* series.

A list of other titles in the *Best Seller Romance* series
can be found at the end of this book.

Elizabeth Hunter

THE TOWER OF THE WINDS

MILLS & BOON LIMITED
LONDON · TORONTO

First published 1973
Australian copyright 1981
Philippine copyright 1981
This edition 1981

© Elizabeth Hunter 1973

ISBN 0 263 73654 7

Set in Linotype Plantin 10 on 11 pt.

Made and printed in Great Britain by Richard Clay (The Chaucer Press) Ltd, Bungay, Suffolk

For
FRANCES PLEASS
who trod the Sacred Way to Delphi in
my company and liked it best of all our
travels.

O glittering, violet-crowned, chanted in song,
Bulwark of Hellas, renowned Athens,
Citadel of the Gods.

Pindar c. 474 B.C.

CHAPTER ONE

ATHENS was just awakening after the long siesta. One by one, the shops of the Plaka came reluctantly to life. The sound of a radio spilling forth the wailing notes of a typically Middle Eastern song was abruptly stilled. The black-clad women, their head-scarves dragged over the lower parts of their faces, turned away from one another, their lengthy gossip at an end, and hurried on homewards to beat the setting sun. It was four o'clock and there was only one week left now before Christmas.

Charity Archer turned her head a little and found herself looking up at the Acropolis. It had a way of being constantly in view, unexpectedly appearing at the end of a street, or peering over the shoulder of a line of buildings, a reminder that the old gods were not yet done with the city. Charity had not yet made her pilgrimage up to the High Place, but she had every intention of going, just as soon as she had met her sister and found out exactly what was happening.

There were three sisters, called, much to their annoyance, Faith, Hope and Charity. Charity was the youngest by many years. Her sisters had married long since, but Charity had stayed at home, first nursing their dying father, and then struggling to keep the family home going because her sisters had thought it might be useful one day when their own families grew up, for neither of them lived in England. Hope had married an American and farmed in West Virginia, loving every minute of it. Faith had rather more romantically fallen in love with a mysterious Greek and had never been seen in England again. How long was it now? It must be five years, Charity thought, since she had last seen her. Five years punctuated by occasional postcards and even more occasional letters.

It had been a letter that had brought Charity to Athens. Charity had been quite unable to make head nor tail of it, but that had not surprised her. Faith had always liked the complicated rather than the simple, the obscure rather than clarity, in anything she had done. It was the sort of ridiculous arrangement she would make, bringing her young sister running from the other end of Europe with only a few directions, none of them clear, as to where she was to stay and where they were to meet.

Charity, who had never been further afield than France, had flown the day before to Athens and hadn't known whether she was on her head or her heels ever since. Even the alphabet was strange and incomprehensible, meaning nothing at all to her. Nor did the language. She had had the address of the hotel she wanted written out by her sister, but nobody had seemed to know where it was. The taxi had taken her first to the Hilton, and then less hopefully to the Grande Bretagne, but Charity had shaken her head at both places, insisting on the address she had been given. The taxi-driver had shrugged and had patted her consolingly on the shoulder. Finally the light had dawned.

'Koukaki!' he had shouted out, as if it were some magic charm. '*Ne, ne,* Koukaki!' And in a few seconds they had drawn up outside the hotel.

A good night's sleep had put new heart into her. She had spent the morning walking from the hotel to the centre of the city. There had been so much to see. She had seen the guards, magnificent and still in their white summer uniforms, outside the royal palace, and she had walked along one of the streets that joined Syntagma (or Constitution) and Omonia (or Harmony) Squares, and back again along another one.

She had been early in getting to the Plaka. She had had lunch at one of the small *tavernas* that in the evening specialize in bouzouki music and dancing, and had asked anyone who had a smattering of English where she could find

8

the Tower of the Winds. Nobody had known. In the end, she had found it for herself, trying to get a better view of the Acropolis. She had known that the old Greek market had lain at the feet of the Acropolis – the *agora*, it was called on her map. What she had not noticed was that there was a second, smaller *agora*, the Roman market, contemptuously dismissed as being late and of not much interest. And there, at one side, was the Tower of the Winds.

Charity, with a rising sense of excitement, had bought a ticket from the sleepy guardian in the booth, and had walked across the rough ground, looking upwards at the strange eight-sided building, each face decorated by the symbol of the wind it represented. They call it in Greek *Oi Aeridhes*, the Windy Ones, and the name has come to include the surrounding square as well. For long it was thought to be the tomb of Socrates. The Turks thought it such and preserved it as a *tekkeh*, or chapel, or it might have suffered the fate of many other ancient pagan buildings and been demolished. Actually it had not been a tomb but an hydraulic clock, built by a Syrian in the first century after Christ. On the east side, a small round tower had been connected to the Clepsydra spring on the Acropolis and had served as a reservoir for the clock. Once there had been a weather-vane surmounting the building, but now there was nothing but the conch of the North wind, the hailstones falling from a shell of the north-east, the fruit and ears of corn of the east, the urn pouring water of the squally South, the flowers of the zephyr breezes of the south-west, and the upturned vase of the dreadful north-westerly.

Charity was so interested in the building that she forgot for a while why she was there. When she remembered, she sat down on a lump of concrete at the foot of the tower and took out her sister's letter, reading it yet again, while she waited.

Dear Charity,
   How would you like to spend Christmas in Athens with

9

me? Something has come up and I need your help. I may as well tell you that I'm leaving Nikos and taking the baby with me, so you'll understand why I can't have you here. I've booked you into a hotel for the time being. Meet me on the 19th, at the Tower of the Winds, at 4 o'clock, and I'll explain everything to you then. You'll find your ticket and everything else you need – including some money! – in the enclosed wallet. I'm relying on you to come! If anything happens to me, I want you to take my child and bring him up in England. I hate Greece and all things Greek, and I can't bear to think of him ever being one. I'll tell you all when I see you.

God bless,
Faith

Charity immediately discounted most of the drama in the letter, but even so her sister sounded desperate and extremely unhappy. Charity sighed, wishing she knew more about the man Faith had married. She knew his name, Nikos Papandreous, and that he came from a very rich family, but she had never seen his photograph and she had certainly never been asked to meet him.

She thought of the short, rather impersonal note she had sent back to her sister and wished that she had made it a warmer missive. She had tried not to let her personal feelings come into it, but she had not quite been able to put aside Faith's postcards that had told her nothing, perhaps especially the one that had come when she had begged her sister to come to their father's funeral. Even Hope had flown over from the States for that, looking comfortable and as fat as butter and so happy that not even death could disturb her contentment in her home.

It was a little after four o'clock now and there was still no sign of Faith. Charity stood up, drawing her coat more closely about her. It was really quite cold, even if this was Greece of the blue skies and endless sun. She climbed down to the lower level of the *agora* and walked briskly amongst the broken columns, trying not to worry. As if Faith was ever on time for anything! But the worry was still there. *Supposing she didn't come?*

Shivering a little, not entirely with cold, some of it was anticipation of the unknown, Charity sat down again and pulled the book she was reading out of her coat pocket. She was determined to stay calm, as she always stayed calm. Faith would come in the end and she would expect to find her sister waiting for her. A hundred different things might have happened to delay her. Perhaps the baby had been sick, or perhaps her husband had come home early and had wanted her company. But no, that last seemed unlikely. *I hate Greece and all things Greek*, she had written, and Nikos Papandreous was certainly Greek.

She had bought the book because it had Apollo in the title and she had been attracted by the picture of the sun-god on the cover. He was seated at his ease, with Poseidon, the Greek god of the sea, beside him, and his twin, Artemis, on his other side. He had his left hand raised, in what gesture it was impossible to see, for the hand was lost, but his other hand lightly grasped the folds of his robe. It was the beauty of the head that was the most appealing thing about it, however. His hair curled in a quite modern style; the nose was straight and Grecian, almost haughty, at variance with the smooth cheeks and the full, very nearly sulky mouth that was almost smiling but not quite. Charity saw from the note inside the cover that the illustration had been taken from the east side of the Parthenon frieze, and promised herself that she would see the original when she finally made her pilgrimage to the top of the Acropolis.

Then she looked up and saw the original coming towards her. His hair curled black and not a honey-coloured gold, and the mouth was certainly not smiling, but the likeness was astonishing. Because of it, she stood up at his coming and stared at him, knowing that she was being most frightfully rude but unable to prevent herself. The last of the sun lit up his face, showing clearly the length of his eye lashes, and the strong modelling of his jaw.

'What is the matter?' he asked her in impeccable English.

Perhaps he was English? But no, with looks like those he had to be Greek. He was Apollo come to life and walking the earth as if he owned it. Silently, she handed him her book. He looked down at the cover and smiled, his teeth gleaming in the golden rays of the dying sun.

'Is he supposed to look like me?' he inquired. She thought it would have been more fitting the other way about. After all, Apollo had come first, and perhaps he still did, haunting Parnassus and his shrine at Delphi and preaching moderation to the immoderate Hellenes.

'I think he does,' Charity said.

He shrugged. 'Perhaps.' He pocketed the book without looking at it again. Charity watched him as he leaned against the bottom of the Tower, his upper lip caught in his teeth, and studied her with a frankness that embarrassed her.

The Greeks are a very curious people, she reminded herself. They always ask personal questions and they like to be in tactile contact with one another, when they aren't endlessly clicking their 'worry-beads'. It didn't mean a thing. And anyway, she was in no position to complain, for she had certainly looked at him!

'Did you come here to meet someone?' he asked suddenly.

She jumped. 'My sister,' she admitted. 'She's late.'

He waved a hand at the setting sun. 'It will soon be dark. If she does not come, what will you do then?'

'I shall wait,' she said.

He looked annoyed with her, but she pretended not to notice. It was no business of his after all! He took the book out of his pocket again and opened it at the fly-leaf. 'Charity

Archer,' he read aloud. 'This is you?'

'Y – yes.'

'Then you are waiting for Faith Papandreous?'

Charity turned impulsively towards him. 'You know her? How is she? Is she coming?'

'No, she is not coming,' he said slowly.

'Then what am I to do?' The unconscious appeal in her voice brought his dark eyes back to her face.

'You will be very brave and accept what I have to tell you,' he said firmly. 'Then you will go back to England and not think of us again. It will be better so.'

Better for whom? She licked her lips. 'Are you – are you Nikos?'

He shook his head, his eyes still holding hers. 'I am afraid not. I am his brother Loukos. You have heard of me, perhaps?'

Charity fiddled helplessly with her fingers. 'My – my sister is not a very good letter-writer.'

'No?' He sounded surprised. 'But surely she wrote some replies to all your letters to her?'

'A few postcards. She – she doesn't like writing letters.'

'And you do?'

'No, but I suppose I had more reason to keep in touch,' Charity said. 'She has a husband and child, whereas I had – very little to occupy—'

'You had your father to nurse,' he interrupted. He seemed to know a great deal about her! 'But I suppose you had less to occupy your heart. But now your father is dead. Is there still no one in your life?'

'I have friends. I may marry—'

'Ah, you have a boy-friend, a fiancé!'

'Well, he hasn't asked me yet. Not that it's any business of yours!' she added crossly. She didn't want to think about Colin right now, in fact she didn't often think about Colin at all, but he thought about her all right, sending her flowers and taking her out to dinner and – and boring her to death!

13

'But you intend to accept him when he does ask you?' Apollo insisted, unimpressed by her rebuke.

'*Yes!*'

'Good, then you will not feel what I tell you so deeply. You have mourned enough in the last year, and the English are not well adapted to tragedy.'

'Who is?' Charity retorted defiantly.

He smiled briefly. 'The Greeks have long understood its meaning. We have a tragic history. We know what it means to be slaves and to have our children taken away from us. What do you know of such things?'

Charity stirred uneasily. 'What is it you want to say to me?'

He held out his hands to her in a simple gesture of sympathy. To her surprise, for she seldom touched people she didn't know well, she found herself responding by placing her own hands in his. The warmth of the contact comforted her.

'It is about your sister. She is dead,' he said.

'But she couldn't be! She told me to meet her here!'

'Perhaps she was coming here,' he said very gently. 'I know only that she quarrelled with Nikos. She got into one of their cars and drove away from his house. Naturally enough, he followed her in another car. I think perhaps he wished to frighten her, by forcing her very close to the edge of the road. She was not a – good driver and she went over the cliff. Nikos followed her. Neither of them were alive when they were found.'

Charity stared at him, disbelief in her eyes. 'Dead? *Both* of them were found dead?'

'I'm afraid so.'

She turned away so that he would not see the devastating effect of his words. She would not give him or anyone else the entrée into her private world of desolation. The Archers had always been a proud family, and that was all she had left to her now, her pride and an aching void in her middle. 'He

14

shouldn't have gone after her,' she said aloud. 'Why couldn't he have left her alone?'

'She was his wife. He had every right to make her return to him.'

Charity took refuge in anger. 'I don't believe you!' she cried out. 'Faith was afraid of him! She wrote and told me so!'

His disapproval cut like a knife through her misery, making her blink. 'She was leaving him!' she declared, but his disapproval only grew stronger and she sought for another weapon to fling at him, to prove that something of her sister lived on in her, that she had not been quenched for all time by the physical fact of her death. 'Where is the baby?' she demanded. 'I'll take him back to England with me!'

'I am afraid not,' Nikos' brother said curtly. 'Alexandros is my responsibility. He is my brother's son and shall be brought up as such.'

'Oh no!' Charity clenched her fists, preparing to do battle. Fighting in her sister's cause was very much better than tears. She did not want this man, who looked like Apollo, to know how alone and bereft she was.

'I am not prepared to argue the matter with you,' he said coldly. 'It is already decided.'

Charity did not often lose her temper, but when she did so she did it thoroughly, without any thought as to the consequences. Now it proved a marvellous relief to the tight knot of agony inside her. She glared up at him, tilting her chin forward to show her determination.

'Then you can undecide it! He is my sister's son and *she* wants him brought up in England, and I intend to do just that! Where is he? I want to see him now, at once!'

'That is impossible!'

'Only because you choose to make it so! I have my sister's letter and I intend to act on her instructions – and it will take more than you to stop me!'

He gave her a brilliant look that passed her by. 'Are you threatening me?' he drawled.

'Yes, I am!'

'I see. I suppose you know you haven't got a leg to stand on?'

'I'm a blood relation! And I can prove that my sister wanted me to have her baby!'

His snort of contempt did little to lessen her anger. 'What good is that going to do you? His father wished the contrary. The boy is Greek!'

'But Faith was his mother!' She swallowed her growing dismay. 'I'll – I'll take you to court if you insist on keeping him!'

His silence was far more distressing to her than anything he could have said. Far from reflecting her own anger, he looked faintly amused and very, very sure of himself.

'You don't think it will do any good?' she hazarded.

He shook his head. 'The boy is Greek. His father's wishes must prevail, even in the courts – even in England, I thin' Your sister was Nikos' wife, the woman of his house, but she had no right to take the child away from his father.'

The woman of his house! What a term to use in connection with Faith, who had always relished her freedom and her independence of others. No wonder she had come to hate Greece!

'But what am I to do? She trusted me to do something!'

Loukos Papandreous stood up. 'It is hard for you just now, but how would it be to start your own marriage with your sister's baby in the house? It is better for you too that the child should stay with me.'

Charity fingered Faith's letter in her pocket. There must be something she could do! If she could see the boy perhaps some inspiration would come to her? It shouldn't be impossible just to take the child and disappear with him back to England. But no, she could not do that. Perhaps his Greek family were fond of him too.

'I want to see him!' she said aloud.

'Alexandros?'

'Of course. Only Faith called him Alexander. I shall too!'

He shrugged. 'As you like. He is too young to be confused quite yet. But, Charity, a word of advice. If I take you to see my parents and on to see the boy at Arachova, you will not try to involve yourself in things which are no affair of yours. Your sister caused my parents a deep hurt and I would not have the wound opened again by you. It will be bad enough for them to know that you are Faith's sister!'

Charity blinked. Her anger had died away, leaving a nagging anxiety that there was something else about Faith that she did not know. Even if her in-laws had been prejudiced against her, and they probably were, she couldn't imagine this man condemning her out of hand. Perhaps it was because she was a woman and a foreigner, and she was beginning to suspect that in Greece this was a chronic disadvantage, that Nikos had been able to blacken his wife's name.

'Faith was a fine person!'

He looked her up and down with an insolence she would not have put up with from an Englishman. 'You are not much like her,' he remarked.

There was no denying that. Faith had been tall and built on the same generous lines as Hope. Her hair had been the colour of burnished copper and her eyes a vivid green. Charity was different. She was not particularly tall, nor particularly anything, except for her hair which was a violent shade of red and gave her a considerable amount of trouble.

'Are you like Nikos?' she retorted.

His laugh took her by surprise. 'Not at all to look at. But you are a little like your sister to look at. You are unlike her in your ways.'

'Thanks very much!'

17

'It was a compliment,' he murmured.

'Then it was a very nasty one! Faith was—' What had Faith been? she wondered. She could really remember very little about her. She had floated through her adolescence, attracting boys to her side with an ease that had caused Hope to agonize over her own attractions and had thus made her less attractive than ever. She had been incredibly selfish about everything. It wasn't that she had tried to do anyone down; she hadn't considered anyone else important enough for that. If she had wanted something, it would never have occurred to her that there was any reason why she shouldn't take it. After all, why should anyone deny her? And her family never had, no matter what it had cost them.

'Yes?' Loukos prompted her.

'Faith was marvellous!' Her enthusiasm wavered into uncertainty, but she picked herself up and hurried on. 'She made life exciting. Events had a way of revolving round her and *everyone* enjoyed themselves more. Oh, you don't understand what she was like!'

'I agree she was a catalyst. Did you enjoy yourself more when she was there?' His brilliant eyes demanded the truth, but she couldn't bring herself to betray Faith by revealing how often her sister had hurt her – and Hope too!

'You sound as though you didn't like her,' she said.

'I didn't.'

She was doubly shocked. Shocked that he hadn't admired Faith as much as every other male of her acquaintance had, and even more shocked that he had said so. One did not, in her experience, say such things about the dead. She gulped and tears started into her eyes. She couldn't believe that Faith was dead! Poor Faith! Had she been afraid of dying as she had been afraid of Nikos?

Loukos did nothing to comfort her. He merely went on looking at her, moving his position slightly so that he had the advantage of the last of the light and she could no longer see his face at all.

'We shall have to go,' he said at last. 'This place closes at sunset. I shall take you back to your hotel—'

'Please don't! I can go by myself!'

'If you wander through the streets of Athens by yourself in the dark you will soon find your motives to be misunderstood! Where are you staying?'

She told him reluctantly the name of her hotel, noticing the distaste with which he received the information. 'I can take a taxi. Nobody will misunderstand that!'

'I have said I will take you, Miss Archer. The hotel is well enough as a place to sleep, but the food there is scarcely adequate. I shall return for you later and we shall have dinner together. We can make our arrangements for to-morrow when I shall take you to Arachova, to see the child. You will want to see Delphi at the same time, yes? It will be quite easy to do both, and it will be convenient to have you with me. I am taking Alexandros to my parents and it is a long drive for a small child, even if he had his nurse with him. It will give you a chance to get to know him!' he added dryly. 'That is what you want, no?'

Charity smiled despite herself. 'I suppose he's car-sick,' she said without rancour.

'So I have been told. You will come?'

She nodded. 'Yes, I'll come. But there is one thing, *kyrie*. Isn't Delphi quite a long way from Athens? Why is Alexander there? I always understood that Faith lived in Athens?'

'Once they did,' he agreed.

'Once?'

'Before Nikos became interested in Greek theatre,' he explained with obvious reluctance. 'There was this American woman – she was married to a Greek – and she did much to revive the ancient theatre at Delphi. As a matter of fact she is buried there, I will show you her grave when we go there tomorrow. Nikos saw one of her productions a long time ago and he wanted to do something similar himself. He took a house at Arachova, which is the village next to Delphi, and went to live there. He planned a great season of drama for next year.' He sighed. 'Now his plans have gone to his grave with him.'

'Oh, what a shame!' Charity exclaimed.

Loukos smiled a bitter smile. 'Faith did not approve of his giving up his business life for a dream. If the baby had not been coming, she would not have gone to Parnassus with him. But she was afraid to be left in Athens by herself. She spoke no Greek.'

'But Nikos' parents were here!'

'They speak very little English. During the war, perforce, they learned a little German, but they are elderly now and see no reason to learn new ways. They have earned their peace, and Nikos would not allow Faith to disrupt it.' He sighed again. 'Now it looks as though she has succeeded despite him. To have a baby in the house is not a good thing when you are past a certain age.'

'Perhaps you should let me have him after all?' Charity put in impulsively. But he only shook his head. He smiled at her though and took her arm, guiding her confidently across the rough ground and out into the square where his car was waiting. He opened the door for her and then went round to the other side, pausing to light himself a cigarette. As the match flared, lighting up his features, Charity remembered her book and she wondered why he had not returned it to her straight away. She waited until he had seated himself and then she asked him for it.

'I want to see what sort of person Apollo was,' she told him.

He was immediately scornful. 'You will not find out from such a book! The gods do not give themselves away so easily!' He started the engine and then turned and looked at her. 'Or were you really hoping to find out more about me?' He handed her the book with a tight grin. 'You will find out far more about us both at Delphi tomorrow. And I shall find

20

out about you!'

Charity's heart missed a beat, but she told herself that she had nothing to be afraid of from Loukos Papandreous. She had no dark secrets for him to discover, whereas he had a great deal of explaining to do before she would be satisfied. Faith had called to her for help and somehow, by hook or by crook, she would settle her sister's account with her husband's family.

'Shall I find out about Nikos too?' she asked.

'Nikos was easy to understand. If you think I resemble Apollo, Nikos certainly had a look of Dionysius. Perhaps that is why he was so interested in theatre. The play began in Dionysius' cult, during the drunken revels that were held in his honour. Nikos liked good wine and a lack of order in his life. He would put on the first clothes that came to hand and laugh if anyone wanted to be serious when he wanted to be gay. It is said that there are two sides to the Greek character, always striving for the upper hand. Apollo and Dionysius still divide us as they seek to extend their rule. It is impossible to serve them both.'

'Dionysius is too disreputable a character for my taste,' Charity said. 'He was Bacchus in the Roman world, wasn't he?'

'The Greek gods are not as cruel as the Roman. You have little to fear from them.'

'I don't,' she denied. 'I don't know enough about them. I've never been much interested in myths. They're so – so unreal!'

'They also explain much. Charity, will you bring your sister's letter with you tonight? I wish to see it. There are things that neither of us know, but that is no reason why we should be enemies.'

Charity sat and thought about it. Her first inclination was to hand over the letter and all the responsibility she felt towards her sister to this stranger, which was strange in itself, for she wasn't sure that she even liked him, and she knew Faith wouldn't have trusted anyone whose name was Papandreous.

'I'll think about it,' she said at last.

She got swiftly out of the car, pausing only to thank him for bringing her back to the hotel.

'I will come for you at half past eight, if that is not too early for you?'

She thought it on the late side herself, but she said nothing, only nodded her consent and hurried away from him into the hotel.

Her room was shuttered and gloomy. She switched on one of the inadequate lights and plumped down on the bed, suddenly exhausted from the emotions of the day. In the next-door room someone was singing a Greek song that had been all the rage in London, five years before, when Faith had first said she was marrying a Greek and was going to live in Greece. Charity couldn't remember the words, though she knew it to be a farewell lament. Oh, Faith, she thought, why did you have to die so young? And she put her hands up to her face and found she was weeping.

CHAPTER TWO

THE trouble with having red hair is that one does not cry gracefully, leaving no sign of the havoc wrought by tears. On the contrary, one emerges from a bout of weeping bearing a strong resemblance to a Victoria plum and feeling worse. Charity did what she could by bathing her face in cold water and thinking bright thoughts, but she still looked awful, even when the dim, unflattering lights of the hotel were taken into consideration.

For a long time she sat on the edge of her bed, which she had found was the best place to look at herself in the looking glass, and wondered what she was to do. She could, she supposed, send a message down to reception to say that she was indisposed, but she had no confidence that Loukos Papandreous wouldn't see fit to come up to see for himself. Yet the idea of eating out with him was not one that appealed to her. She wasn't ready yet to face him. She wanted to come to some decision first, and how could she, when all she could think about was that awful moment when Faith had gone over the cliff at the edge of the road and had fallen to her death.

Half past eight found her downstairs, however, because anything else seemed to be more and more impossible. She occupied herself by looking at the postcards and the fancy key-rings that the hotel sold to their guests, so she didn't see Loukos Papandreous come into the hotel.

'*Kalispera*, Kyria Charity.'

She jumped and turned, forgetting for a moment her resolution to stay in the shadows.

'Good evening. *Kalispera*,' she whispered back.

He had changed his clothes and was now dressed for the evening. The resemblance to Apollo was more marked than ever, though the electric lighting made a poor substitute for the sun.

'I – I think you ought to call me Miss Archer,' she added. 'We don't know each other after all.'

His eyebrows rose. 'I have told you my name, Loukos. I make you free of it. Archer is too military a name for you. I think an Archer would not spend the evening crying. Faith would not have done so, so why should you cry for her?'

'She was my sister – and I loved her!'

His expression softened, giving her a jolt because she didn't want his sympathy – *anyone's* sympathy just at that moment. She was so afraid that she would disgrace herself and burst out crying all over again.

'Yes, of course she was your sister,' he agreed. 'It is fitting that you should mourn for her. But mourn for the girl that she was, not the woman she had become, for she was someone you did not know—'

'Of course I knew my own sister!' Charity exclaimed.

He smiled slightly. 'How many years were there between you? Ten?'

'Eight,' she admitted. 'But Hope is only one year younger than Faith, and she knew her too!'

Loukos bit back whatever it was he had been about to say. 'Shall we go?' he said instead.

Charity hesitated. 'I think I'd rather go back to my room. I m-may start to cry again, and I don't want to embarrass you.'

He didn't look as though he would be easily embarrassed, but what man could possibly want to escort her throbbing face anywhere? She stepped further back into the shadows and attempted a small, shy smile.

'No,' he said positively. 'You are not going to cry any more. There will be no time for that! We shall be very gay and think only of the future.' A smile crept into his eyes. 'This may be the last holiday you will have by yourself before you marry, have you thought of that? I shall do my

24

best to show you all that you are going to miss!'

Charity cast him a startled look. 'Oh, but—' she began.

'How long did you plan to stay in Athens?' he asked her.

'I don't know. Over Christmas at least. But I don't know that I shall stay – now.'

Loukos placed her wrap around her shoulders and led her out from the hothouse atmosphere of the hotel into the cool night. 'Why don't you ask your young man to come out here to you for Christmas?'

Colin? Out here? She was shaken by the very idea. It would be fun to have someone with whom to see the sights, but she felt that it would also involve a commitment to him that she was far from ready to make quite yet.

'I don't know,' she said.

He put her in the car, his brilliant eyes meeting hers. 'Because you're not sure? Or because you still think that you may be taking Alexandros home with you?' he challenged her.

Her eyes dropped to the dashboard. 'I don't think that's any business of yours!' she claimed.

'But I mean to know! You are not having Alexandros, Miss Archer. You will be far happier when you have faced up to that.'

'Then I'll ask Colin if he'd like to come to Athens. Only the fare isn't cheap and – and I don't know how he's placed just at the moment.' She thought herself that she might well have been thinking of Colin's pocket when she had hesitated, but Loukos Papandreous was not deceived.

'I shall be interested to see this young man of yours,' he said. 'I will invite you both to my house some time over the holiday. It will be good for him as he knows that your father is dead and that you have no brother.'

Charity was robbed of speech for a long moment. Could he really be intending to vet her boy-friend? And if so, why? She was nothing to him, and she had been making all her

25

own decisions for more years than she liked to count.

'Don't you ever mind your own business?' she asked.

But Loukos only laughed. 'Is he so impossible?' he countered.

'Of course not!' she denied with some heat.

'Then why should you object?'

She strove to find the words to tell him, words that he could not possibly misunderstand, that she ran her own life and would not thank him to tell her what to do whatever his intentions.

'I've known Colin for years!' was what she actually said. 'I know him as well as I know anyone!'

'Of course. But, Kyria Charity, you are a woman and cannot possibly see him in quite the same way as a man will. You must allow me to do this for you. We are connected by your sister's marriage to my brother, so it is perfectly proper for me to ensure that this Colin will be a suitable husband for you. You must tell me all about him while we eat.'

Charity had no intention of doing anything of the sort. She flounced round in her seat and studied the Christmas lights that decorated the streets of Athens. It was a curious thing about Athens, she thought, that it seemed to be in the wrong place. It had a look of a modern German city, without any of the Greek grace that pictures of the Parthenon and other Greek ruins had led her to expect. It was a bourgeois city, full of blocks of apartments and small family shops. Department stores, such as she was used to in London, seemed to be non-existent.

'It doesn't look Greek,' she said, forgetting her anger with her companion.

'Perhaps because it was laid out by Bavarian architects,' he answered. 'Our first king in modern times was a Bavarian prince, King Otto. His queen laid out the gardens by the old royal palace. You must visit them. They are very beautiful.'

'Am I to be allowed out with Colin by myself?' she asked, her voice dripping sarcasm. 'I can hardly believe it!'

'It will depend—'

'On what?' she flashed back.

He cast her one of his brilliant looks. 'On what this Colin is like, for one thing. And on what you are like, for another.'

He touched her hand in a brief moment of contact. 'Faith should have insisted that you came to Greece as soon as your father died. It was not right to leave you alone, with no one to protect you. I cannot approve! Where have you been living?'

Charity bit her lip. 'In my father's house,' she told him.

'Which is now yours?'

'Well, no, not exactly. It belongs to all three of us.'

'Then you will not be living there when you marry?'

He was way ahead of her. She frowned thoughtfully in the darkness. 'I haven't thought about it. I hope not! It's a large, depressing place, with huge, very dark rooms downstairs and a vast number of freezing bedrooms upstairs.'

'But this Colin would like to live there?'

Charity was annoyed by Loukos' persistence. What did it matter where Colin wanted to live? 'I shouldn't think so,' she muttered.

He parked the car neatly in the square by the Tower of the Winds and came round to her side of the car, opening the door for her. As she stepped out, he put his hand beneath her chin and tipped up her face to meet the light from the lamp above them.

'No more tears,' he said very gently. 'No more sadness, for this evening at least. Is it a pact?'

She smiled weakly. 'No more tears,' she agreed. '*I have wept for these things once already.*'

'So?' he teased her. 'You are a scholar also that you can quote from our Greek plays? Can you also name the author?'

27

That was a much harder task. 'I think it may be Euripides,' she said, stepping away from him, because she was more conscious than she liked of his firm touch under her chin.

His brilliant look rested lightly on her face. 'Did you learn our plays at school?'

'No. I'm ashamed to say that I've read hardly any of them. That was a flash in the pan. It came into my mind and out it came!'

'Ah!' he laughed. 'It was your red hair speaking! I like it better when you forget to consider every word that you say.'

He might, but she preferred a decent reserve when she was speaking to one who was still a stranger to her. He began to walk down one of the narrow streets of the Plaka, now alive with bouzouki music and laughter. His breadth of shoulder and his air of certainty were very tempting to her. How nice it would have been if she could have relied on him, but she couldn't. She hadn't yet determined whether he was friend or foe, but she suspected that, as far as Faith was concerned, he was the latter, and that made him her enemy too.

'*Kyrie*, it's kind of you to concern yourself with my affairs, but I've looked after myself for a long time now. I prefer it that way—'

He turned his head, dismissing her careful speech with a contemptuous gesture. 'No woman can prefer it that way!'

'But I do!'

He shrugged. 'It is of no moment.' He held out his hand to her. 'Come, Charity, you must be hungry and we have many things to discuss before we go to Arachova and Delphi in the morning.'

She hurried after him. 'Oh? What?' she asked him.

'To begin with I still wish to read your sister's letter. You have it with you?'

28

She nodded. 'Loukos, what are you going to do with little Alexander? I think I have a right to know that at least before I go back to England.'

For once he avoided her gaze and she knew that the question was unwelcome to him. 'When the decision has been made you will certainly be told,' he answered stiffly. 'I will not forget that you are the boy's aunt and will wish to see him from time to time, but it is I who will decide his future.'

'Won't you even discuss it?' she begged.

'I see no reason to do so. If this Colin is the man you say he is, he may be useful when we come to a decision. That is why I wish him to come here.'

'But it has nothing to do with Colin!' she protested. 'And it has a great deal to do with me!'

He came to a standstill, frowning fiercely at her. 'I thought you were thinking of marrying this man?'

'What if I am?'

Loukos spread his hands in a comprehensive gesture. 'When he is your husband, he will naturally take command of your affairs, and so it is better that he should play his part from the beginning.'

'But you don't understand!'

He silenced her with a movement of his hand. '*Ftáni pyá!* That will do! A pretty woman should have better things to do than to quarrel over things she should not be worried about. And you are a very pretty woman!'

She was startled into silence. She was, of course, extremely angry that he should patronize her, and dismiss her opinions for no other reason than that she was a woman, but she couldn't help a sneaking excitement that he should think her pretty. *Very pretty*, he had said, and if he thought so now when her eyes were all bloated from the tears she had shed, he must really think that she was a little good-looking.

She followed him into the *taverna*, blinking at the lights,

29

noise, and zest for living that filled the crowded tables all about her. A waiter came forward with a smile and showed them to a table, his words of greeting completely drowned in the fever of activity with which the dancers threw themselves into the dance of the moment. Loukos smilingly accepted a menu and gave a rapid order before handing the card back to the waiter. Charity, resigned to not being consulted, looked about her with interest, catching the eye of the young boy who ran from table to table, bringing their orders for wine and ouzo from somewhere down the street. He kissed his hand to her and she averted her eyes as if she had been stung. Good heavens, she thought, he couldn't have been a day older than twelve!

Loukos gave her a look of amusement which embarrassed her still further. 'What did I tell you? He, too, thinks you are pretty!'

'He ought to be at school!' she choked.

He laughed out loud. 'A Greek will tell a woman that she pleases him when he is still in the cradle!'

'Really?' she said softly. 'And what about her? She must be very confused to find herself suddenly desirable, if her opinion is ignored as if she were a fool at all other times!'

Loukos grinned. 'There is a difference, but it is not for me to point it out to you. Nor do I consider you a fool, Charity Archer, but I will allow that you are confused! Too much has happened to you today. You will feel better when you have had a good night's sleep, and not nearly so tetchy.'

'*Tetchy?*' she repeated, wondering where he had learned such a word. 'Let me tell you, I've been a model of sweet reason! Whereas you—! You're impossible! I don't believe even the Greeks—'

His eyes were brighter than ever. 'Yes, Miss Archer?'

'Oh, you don't listen to anything I say!' she objected.

'It is hard to concentrate on your words when the look in your eyes is saying something much more interesting! Naturally it will occur to any Greek how pleasant it would be to

30

make love to you, but for the moment you are safe with me, and not because you have been crying, but because you are alone and have no means to protect yourself. Does that satisfy you?'

She stared at him, wide-eyed. 'Am I supposed to be complimented?'

He shrugged, amused. 'As you like,' he drawled.

Well, really! But it was she who looked away first, feeling suddenly breathless and very, very conscious of the appreciation in his dark eyes. She found herself wondering what it would be like to feel his mouth on hers, to touch the smooth brown of his skin, even to feel his arms about her. It was a very disturbing thought, and one she had never caught herself thinking before. Indeed, she was more than a little shocked that such improper notions about any man should have crept up on her and taken her by storm, for now it was in her mind she couldn't get it out again, and she was almost sure that he knew it.

'You – you wanted to see my sister's letter,' she reminded him hastily, determined to change the conversation. She searched in her bag and drew out the letter, pushing it across the table to make sure that there was no chance of their fingers touching. 'You can see how frightened she was. *And* that she wanted me to have Alexander!'

He read the letter without looking at her, a slight frown between his eyes. 'Very dramatic!' he commented. 'Is this the only letter you've had from her, or did she leave one for you at your hotel?'

She was surprised at the question. 'But it says I was to meet her at the Tower of the Winds. She was going to tell me everything then, so why should she write to me again? Besides, she didn't like writing letters.'

He handed her back the letter. 'She must have had great confidence in you,' he remarked. 'There is no address for you to write back to.'

'But I had her address— I mean, I had an Athens address

31

that I always wrote to. I didn't know she was living somewhere else.'

'In Arachova? I wonder why she didn't tell you. They had sold their apartment in Athens nearly a year ago. It was fortunate that your letter was delivered to me and that I opened it. I had already been through all my brother's papers and I recognized your writing on the envelope—'

'But I never wrote to Nikos!'

The twinkle of amusement came back into his eyes. 'Your sister shared his desk,' he told her. 'All your letters were there, interspersed with bills and other letters to do with Nikos' work.'

'Oh,' said Charity. 'I hadn't thought that he might read them!'

'Why not? He *was* Faith's husband.'

'I suppose you've read them too!' she went on crossly. 'Well, it wasn't my fault that they didn't say much. Faith never told me what she was doing, so they were bound to be a bit one-sided.'

'Will you believe me that I didn't mean to read them at first? I wanted your address to let you know about your sister, but you write well and I found I wanted to know more about you.'

Charity sighed and then she smiled. 'As long as you realize you had no right to read them!'

'Only the last one,' he consented. 'It would not have done to have left you waiting at the Tower of the Winds for ever. There is no need to wonder what you said in those other letters, they spoke only of your father's illness, and of the house where you lived. Did you have no fun, Charity, in all those years?'

'Of course I did!' she protested. 'My father was very ill right at the end, but before that—' She broke off, seeing the taut look on his face. 'What's the matter?' she asked him.

He dismissed her enquiry with a twisted smile. 'I was thinking, that's all. It seems to me you were very young to

32

have to shoulder so much responsibility. Is there no one else in your family who could have helped you?'

'I have a bachelor uncle, my father's brother, but I haven't seen him for years! And I wasn't so very young!' she added. An imp of mischief lit up her warm, sherry-brown eyes. 'There was Colin, of course.'

Loukos nodded. 'Of course. I had forgotten him. No doubt that was why Nikos didn't fly to England when your father died.' He smiled at her across the table. 'I am glad you had this Colin to make all the arrangements for you. It is not right for a woman to have to do these things.'

Charity felt the warm colour suffuse her cheeks, but she said nothing. How could she possibly tell him that Colin had been away on business at the time and that even if he had been there, he wouldn't have dreamed of interfering with something that he would have considered to be wholly her business? It was difficult, though, not to think how pleasant it would have been for someone else to have taken the immediate decisions out of her hands at that particular time. There had been so much to do, and she had hated it – all of it!

Fortunately, Loukos was busy talking to the wine-boy and didn't see the confusion on Charity's face. She didn't approve of making comparisons between people, but it was difficult not to remember how Colin had concluded that she would cope, not only with her own problems, but often with his as well; whereas Loukos might not consult her about what she wanted to eat – or drink! – but he took charge of other things as well. It seemed there were two sides to what she had first thought was merely arrogance on his part.

He looked up, satisfied by his final choice of wine, and smiled at her. 'I think unresinated wine until you are used to it,' he said. 'I am told it is an acquired taste.'

'But if you prefer it,' she protested, 'I'd like to try it.'

He shook his head. The decision had already been made. 'If you wish to try it, I shall order it for you in Delphi. The

Parnassus water is so delicious that it will not matter if you prefer not to drink the wine!'

She made no objection at all. She even *liked* him to decide the matter for her. And that worried her. She set her mind to fretting at the problem until she could solve it to her own satisfaction and, up to a point, she did. It was because she was still numb from the news of her sister's death and didn't much care about anything. Yes, that was it! Only she didn't feel half as badly as she had felt earlier in the evening, and that was thanks to him too. He had given her something else to think about. Well, she had *felt* something, at any rate. In fact she had felt a great deal. She eyed him covertly from under her eyelashes and wondered at herself. If this was the effect Greece had on her, the sooner she was returned to the safety of home and Colin the better it would be!

'Wasn't it Apollo who held the three graces in the hollow of his hand?' she asked aloud.

His laughter suddenly burst out of him as if she had kicked him. He doubled up with mirth, his great laugh ringing out across the restaurant. Charity thought it was excessive. She imagined that everyone would be looking at them, staring in astonishment at the noise he made, but it soon became clear, even to her, that to all but her this was considered quite normal behaviour from anyone trying to have a good time. What reason was there to keep one's voice down and mutter in one's beard, if one felt like shouting with laughter, or joining in the non-stop song and dance? It was as if the Greeks had to constantly prove to themselves that they were alive and intended to make the most of it.

'My dear girl, I must assure you that I am not Apollo, no matter if you do think I look like him! I am Loukos Papandreous! Isn't that enough for you?'

She drew her dignity about her, even more disturbed by that arrogant announcement. *I am Loukos Papandreous!* She tried to imagine herself declaiming that she was Charity Archer in the same tone of voice, but her mind boggled. She

34

wasn't that sure that she was anyone in particular, and she envied him his certainty.

'Anyway,' he went on, 'I think the Graces was only another name for the Fates, and I don't think I'd like to have much to do with them. But there is a statue of Apollo somewhere, stark naked, with the three Graces standing on his hand. They were apt to trail after him, poor dears. I expect it was because they were something to do with the moon in her death-aspect—'

'Oh yes,' Charity said brightly. 'He would rather outshine them when he came up in the morning. Poor things, as you say!'

'They had the nights in which to weave their spells, as women do. It is only when the sun comes up that a man must go about his own business.'

'Leaving the women behind them?'

'Why, yes, if they will stay there. Most of them, I have found, are more interested in Apollo than waiting for the darkness to come again. Even you wish to make your pilgrimage to his shrine tomorrow. Would you wait quietly in Athens for me to bring the baby back for you to see?'

'You promised I could go with you!' she protested. He didn't know how much she wanted to go to Delphi! It was nothing to do with her sister, or any of the things that had happened since she had come to Athens. It was a dream that had haunted her as ever since she had first read that people had gone to that one spot for perhaps five thousand years. She had always wanted to know why, sure that its secret would be revealed to her if she could see it for herself.

'If you don't take me,' she said, 'I'd trail after you like – like Nemesis!'

'Does it mean so much to you?' he asked her. There was an inscrutable look on his face.

'Yes,' she said. 'It's silly, I know, but I've always wanted to go to Delphi.'

'Then go you shall.' He reached out a hand to her, crush-

35

ing her fingers in his strong grasp. 'I hope you won't be disappointed.'

Charity felt quite muzzy with noise and wine when he took her back to her hotel. Her eyes were drooping with fatigue and she didn't dare to look at her watch to see what the time was in case it was as late as she suspected. She had learned a lot about the Greeks in one evening, she thought. She had learned that they never slept, for a start! And that they had a zest for living that made her long to throw her bonnet over the nearest windmill and join them.

She had learned something about Loukos Papandreous too. He had told her that he was a business man, with the usual interests in shipping and olives, but it was not that that had interested her. She had learned something about herself too, and that was something she wanted to think about for a long time all by herself. It had to do with the wine-boy who, if Loukos was to be believed, had compared her hair to the rays of the sun, and who had expected her to enjoy his enjoyment of his discovery as much as he did. It had a whole lot more to do with the way Loukos had looked at her, and danced with her, and had kissed her hand when they parted. It had all added up to a strange sensation that she had never consciously felt before. She had felt feminine and glad to be so.

Colin, whom she thought she loved, had never made her feel that her sex was a precious, lovely thing, a gift from the gods. No one had. But tonight it had all been different and, despite her tears and her misery at her sister's death, she had caught a glimpse of what life was all about and she couldn't be sad any longer.

Tomorrow, she thought, she would think again about Faith, and Faith's son, and whether she could trust Loukos or not, but just for tonight, she would dream her dreams and be glad she was alive, as Loukos was. She stared at herself in the glass for a long moment and was surprised to see there

36

were no traces left of the tears she had shed. Her eyes were as brilliant as his were when they laughed at some joke. Oh, Charity Archer, she said to herself, this was no time to go on some voyage of discovery to goodness knows where! She was going to need all her wits about her to carry out Faith's dying wishes, and that was what she was there for!

She turned out the light and pulled the blankets about her, determined to have some firm plan of campaign before she saw Loukos again. But she was asleep from the moment she set her head on the rock-hard pillow and tried to summon up her powers of concentration. She remembered thinking something rather pleasant about the next day – and then there was only a blessed nothingness.

CHAPTER THREE

DELPHI! *'The shrine that is the centre of the loudly echoing earth'*, as Pindar described it. Charity stared at the ruins that nestled into the steep cliffs of the mountain behind them, cliffs that had been known for centuries as the Shining Ones. It was hard to see why they had been so named in the light, drizzling rain that blew through the valley. Their summit pierced the cloud that had been caught against their craggy heights. Below the clouds were the ruins themselves, the theatre, the six remaining pillars of the Temple of Apollo, and the Sacred Way, lined by the various treasuries representing all the different parts of Greece, up which the pilgrims had made their way to consult the famous oracle.

Loukos drew the car into the side of the road and let her look her fill. 'The ruins further down, on the other side of the road, is where the pilgrims waited for the required three days before they could go up to the oracle,' he told her. 'The Temple there was dedicated to Athene and was known as Athene Pronaea. In the spring you can find hyacinths and bee-orchis growing wild there. It was down there that the athletes practised for the Pythian Games, which were held every four years up in the stadium above the theatre.'

'Why Pythian?' Charity asked.

'Because before Apollo made the sanctuary and oracle his own, it was dominated by the Python who had pursued Leto, Apollo's mother, because Hera, who was Zeus's official wife, was jealous of her and was determined that she should have no resting place in which to bear Apollo and his twin sister Artemis. Later, Apollo killed the Python and took over guardianship of the oracle. The Games were held every year at one of four sites. Olympia is the most famous today, but all four were considered equally prestigious in those days.

38

But because the Games only came to each site once every four years then, today the Olympic Games are held only every four years just the same.'

Charity had to confess that she was more interested in the oracle than in the Games. She could scarcely conceal her eagerness to see everything at once. The most beautiful of the ruins at first sight was a completely circular building down by the Temple of Athene. Loukos told her it had once housed the snakes that had symbolized Apollo's interest in medicine.

'There was a good reason for making the pilgrims wait for their turn to visit the oracle,' he said. 'When we go up to the Temple you will be able to see the traces of the secret path that the priests took to visit the applicants below and find out what they were going to ask the oracle when their turn came. It was a very flourishing business, you see, and they wished to make sure of their profits by having their answers ready.'

'But it couldn't always have been like that!' Charity objected. 'I don't believe it!'

'The person I feel sorry for was the poor girl who had to mouth the oracles, sitting in a dank cave on her stool, half drugged by chewing bay-leaves—'

'I thought they were laurel leaves. Daphne, whom Apollo loved and pursued, was turned into a laurel tree. He sadly picked the leaves and they became associated with him and were put about the brows of victors. I'm sure it was a laurel tree!'

'Sweet laurel,' he said, 'which is a bay tree.'

'Oh,' said Charity, reluctant to abandon the argument. 'Do let's go and see where the oracle was! If you're ready?' she added, conscious that he might not be sharing her impatience to visit the famous shrine.

He drove the car to the foot of the actual shrine, parking it in the space provided. Charity hurried up the steps ahead of him. She could hardly bear to wait while he bought their entrance tickets, so anxious was she to set her steps on the age-old Sacred Way that zigzagged its way upwards.

'You will miss something if you are in too much of a hurry,' Loukos teased her. 'First you must look at the treasuries on the way up. Depending from where you came from, you would offer your gift to your own treasury before you went on up to the Temple.'

Obediently, she agreed to pause at the Syphnian Treasury, the fabulous frieze of which is now in the museum, and at the restored Athenian Treasury where Loukos would have left his own gift if he had come two or three thousand years before. He pointed out the ruts that had been carved in the stones beneath their feet to stop the animals from slithering about as they were taken up to be sacrificed at the altar just outside the temple. Charity was dismayed by the thought of the animals being forced up the slope to their death and she looked away quickly, unwilling to dwell on their sufferings.

'If they shivered, they were considered unworthy and their lives were spared,' Loukos comforted her.

'What happened to them then?' Charity demanded.

He shrugged his shoulders. 'I don't know,' he admitted. 'I can't imagine the avaricious priests allowing many animals to escape their grasp!' He laughed at the expression on Charity's face, putting a hand lightly on her shoulder. 'Don't think about it, if it upsets you, though the end result of a modern abattoir is exactly the same! You will be more interested in this containing wall,' he smiled. 'Directly above is the Temple. The Athenians built a kind of verandah along the side of the wall in which they displayed the spoils they had captured from Sparta in the Peloponnesian War. But just look how this wall was built! You see how all the pieces fit one another? This is typically Greek. No mortar was ever used in Greek building, that was an innovation introduced by the Romans. But the wall is interesting for another reason. It is covered in writing, giving details of

40

the various expenses and so on of the shrine. It is rather like a very ancient newspaper and has been of incomparable value to the archaeologists.'

Charity didn't see the writing at first, not until she came right up against the wall, but then she could see that it was covered from end to end in the tiny hieroglyphs of the Greek script. Loukos read out some of the words to her, but in so long a time the language had changed considerably and, mostly, he could only guess at the meaning.

When they climbed up to the Temple itself, he left her to her own devices, for which she was grateful. She needed time to look about her and to tune herself into the meaning of this ancient sanctuary.

'There isn't much left of it,' was all he said before he moved away. 'And what there is is the remains of three Temples. One was destroyed by earthquake, the second by fire. The last was pulled down by Christians who tried to destroy all the old pagan shrines. The three scourges of God, one might say!'

Charity climbed up and down between the different floor levels, looking upwards towards the Shining Ones, and down to the waving branches of a sea of olive trees that could be counted in thousands rather than hundreds. She found the place where Pythia, the name given to the woman who mouthed the oracles, had actually sat on her three-legged throne. The area had been filled in now to stop the more boisterous tourists from jumping down into the area and ruining the ancient floor and walls. The stone on which the Pythia had sat lay beside the Temple now, the three holes into which the legs of the stool had fitted separated from another hole through which the vapours had poured upwards, surrounding the girl, by a gully through which the sacred waters had run, brought all the way from the sacred fountain higher up on the slopes of Parnassus.

Charity sat on the edge of the Temple with her feet on the stone and felt more peaceful about her sister's death. The

41

long drive from Athens had been haunted by the knowledge that they would be passing the actual spot where Faith had met her death. Loukos had driven the whole way in a near-silence. True, he had pointed out the spot where the luckless Oedipus had unknowingly killed his father, before going on to Thebes to answer the riddle of the Sphinx that was terrorizing the city and mounting the throne of his father by marrying his own mother, Jocasta. She had shivered when she had seen what a long way down it was from the new road, that was even now being widened, to the ancient meeting of the roads below.

'Was it near here?' she had asked Loukos, and he had nodded, but he had never told her exactly where it had been, and there were so many earth-moving vehicles being used on the narrow ledge along which the road ran that it was impossible to see any sign of the double tragedy that had killed both Faith and her husband.

Charity thought about her now, and her letter which had brought her hurrying to Greece. Her own life had always been like that, she thought. She had hurried from one to another of her family, picking up the odd pieces of their lives, but she had never had much life of her own to live. She wanted to be someone in her own right, to follow a path of her own, for good or ill, so that she too could hold her head high and claim, 'I am Charity Archer!' Was that too much to ask now that her father and one of her sisters were dead, and there was only Hope who had no need of her?

She went to the edge of the shrine and picked a piece of laurel that she found growing there and placed it on the rock at her feet for a tribute to Apollo. She had nothing else to bring him, unless he wanted her money. Perhaps he liked to be bribed? She knew that some saints had that reputation. How often would St. Anthony refuse to find one's lost property until he had seen the colour of one's money? She smiled at the thought and tucked a twenty-drachmae piece under a corner of the stone where it could not be seen.

She looked up and saw Loukos looking down at her. 'Did you get your answer?' he asked her.

'I don't know,' she said. She smiled uncertainly, surprised to discover that the cloud had lifted to let through a single ray of sunlight. She might not know if she had found an answer, but she had seen Apollo! An oddly human Apollo, who held out his hands to her and drew her up on to the Temple floor beside him. An Apollo lit by sunlight, like a halo about his head, and who smiled at her.

'Come and have a look at the theatre,' he said.

He held her by the hand as they walked up the short distance to the theatre. The sun was getting stronger by the minute and the cliffs took on a new aspect, grey and green, with splashes of terracotta, magnificent in their arrogance. Loukos followed her gaze up to their summit.

'It was from there that they forced Aesop to jump to his death. That's what they did to people who committed the sacrilege of doubting their powers! Or, worse still, embezzled their money!'

'*Aesop*? Aesop, who wrote the fables?'

'The very same. Later on, they found he was not guilty after all and paid compensation to his grandson, but that didn't help poor Aesop!'

So others had fallen over the cliffs to their death, just like Faith. They always had!

'It's a terrible way to die!' she exclaimed.

He squeezed her hand. 'One would know very little about it. It's a pity though that this theatre won't come alive for the whole of next summer as Nikos had planned. It's an incomparable position, isn't it?'

She had to admit that it was. It had looked quite small from down below, and indeed it had only thirty-three tiers of seats, rising in a semi-circle from the stage below. Charity ran lightly up the steps and sat down somewhere near the top, the whole shrine spread out beneath her and, below that, the whole deep valley. She looked shyly down at Loukos.

43

'I suppose,' she hazarded, 'I suppose you wouldn't say something, would you?'

He laughed and she could hear him clearly. He searched for the small cross on the ground that marked the centre of the stage and stood astride it, his head thrown back so that he could watch her expression. Then he laughed again and said something in Greek which she could not understand.

'Shall I translate?' he asked unnecessarily and, without waiting for her answer, went on in English, '*Tell the Emperor that the bright citadel is fallen to the ground. Apollo hath no longer any shelter, or oracular laurel tree, or speaking fountain. Even the vocal stream has ceased to flow.*'

She vaguely recognized the oracular answer Delphi had sent to the Emperor Julian the Apostate, who had tried to return the Roman Empire to paganism, but her whole being rejected it. She was on her feet and clattering down the steps towards Loukos.

'No! *No!* I won't believe it! It's still here for those who can feel it. There *must* be something left after all those ages when people came here in faith.'

He put his arm right round her and held her close. 'Perhaps for some people it is still here. I hope it is for you. It means a lot to you, doesn't it?'

'Yes, it does,' she said and, becoming conscious of his arm about her, she freed herself without looking at him. 'Anyway, I could hear beautifully. Thank you very much.'

'Think nothing of it,' he said indifferently.

The sun had gone in again when they returned to the car and the Shining Ones had returned to their gloomy aspect of winter, grey and forbidding, guarding their captured clouds with aloof grandeur. The misty rain slowly descended into the valley, catching them up just as Charity was turning in her seat to see the last of the broken shrine.

'Cheer up,' Loukos said. 'We'll come back after lunch for

a quick look at the museum. The village of Delphi is just around the corner, but we must go back to Arachova. They are expecting us there for lunch.'

She put her head on one side, glancing across at him. 'Thank you for bringing me here,' she said. 'I shall never forget it.'

The road curved round the mountains, rising sharply towards its highest point which is the picturesque village of Arachova that cascades down the steep slopes, the roof of one house lying at the same level as the ground floor of the one behind it. Loukos kept his eyes firmly on the road ahead of them.

'Why do you worry so, Charity?' he asked her. 'What answer are you seeking from the oracle?'

She twisted her fingers together. 'You wouldn't understand,' she said. 'I don't really understand myself.'

'You may get a double-edged answer. Have you thought of that?'

She nodded. 'It won't matter. I shall still be glad I came!'

By the time they came to Arachova, the rain had changed to sleet. The road was lined on either side by shops selling the handwork of the local women. Highly coloured blankets, bedspreads, and carpets hung in groups from every available corner in front of the shops. Those that were furthest out declared that their goods were all going at half price because of the road widening scheme, but the more central ones could rely on the coach trade and were anyway less affected by the mud and the general inconvenience.

Loukos parked the car where it could do no harm. 'We have to walk from here. Will you be warm enough?'

Charity said she would be. She had no thicker coat to put on even if she had wanted to. She stepped out of the car and grimaced at the biting cold that met her, made worse by the freezing wind that blew up and down the stepped alleys that led from one row of houses to the next. Loukos took her arm

45

and rushed her up one of these alleys, bidding her watch her feet for donkeys, chickens, and even pigs went by the same way.

'Nikos liked the view,' he explained, as they arrived, puffing and panting, at the top.

It was understandable, Charity supposed, but she couldn't help wondering how Faith had coped, carrying the shopping and anything else they needed up and down that hill to the street below.

'Is this the house?' Charity asked. She could hardly believe it. The whole of the ground floor was taken up for use as the stables-cum-pigsty, occupied by a single donkey who poked his way, stiff-legged, across the uneven floor to look at them.

Loukos didn't bother to answer. He led the way up an external flight of stone steps to the living quarters above, calling out something in Greek. A door creaked open and an elderly woman peered over the stone banisters, her face lined with suspicion and hostility that evaporated only when she saw who it was.

'Ah, Kyrie Loukos, it is you! I thought it might be another. I have heard that I may expect another visitor today.'

'Do I know her?' Loukos returned.

The woman nodded, drawing her black scarf more closely around her face. 'You are knowing Thespinis Ariadne Vouzas,' she snapped.

They had spoken in Greek, but Charity recognized that the woman was telling Loukos about some woman and she wondered at his thunderous expression. He said nothing about the woman to Charity, however.

'Will you see the child first, or would you like to eat?'

'I'd like to see Alexander.'

He spoke to the woman who smiled unexpectedly, revealing a mouthful of crowded, blackened teeth. 'It seems you said the right thing,' Loukos said dryly. 'This woman is

Alexandros' nurse. She has been looking after both the boy and the house. She is a local woman and very reliable.'

Charity nodded to the woman and waited as patiently as she could while the nurse went into the bedroom and came back with the baby in her arms. The child was sleeping, but he opened his eyes as Charity held out her arms to receive him and yawned at her. He was warm and smelt of milk and talcum powder, but it was not that that brought the tears starting to her eyes as she looked at him. It was the fact that he was as redheaded as she was herself, with a bright carroty fluff on the top of his head and bronzed eyelashes guarding his perfectly formed eyes. She looked accusingly at Loukos.

'He's every inch an Archer!' she exclaimed.

'But his name is Papandreous,' he reminded her abruptly. 'I'll thank you to remember that!'

'I don't suppose you'll allow me to forget it! But you can't change his looks!' Her face softened as she returned her gaze to her little nephew. 'He's very like Faith, isn't he?'

He came and looked over her shoulder. 'Not particularly. If he's like anyone, I'd say he was more like you. Faith's colouring lacked your brightness.'

Charity laughed. 'That's one way of putting it! I'm afraid she and Hope used up all the family looks long before I arrived! All that was left for me was flame-coloured hair and a hot temper to match!'

'And a warm heart,' he drawled, 'to match the warmth of your eyes.'

She gave him a startled look and then wished she hadn't, for the amusement on his face was unsettling and brought a mist before her eyes, making her suddenly wonder what it would be like to feel that face against hers. She gave herself a mental shake, aware that her hands were shaking and that, between them, they had woken the baby and he was in two minds as to whether to have a good cry or not. She rocked him gently, hiding her face in his shawl, and addressing him

47

softly in English.

'Come,' Loukos commanded, 'it is time we ate. The baby will wait.'

'But he's a *darling*! I wish – I mean, I know he's a Papandreous as well, but I wish he were mine!'

Loukos raised his eyebrows. 'You will have babies of your own. Then perhaps you will feel differently about him.'

'*Never!*' she declared.

His amused look made her feel a fool. She returned the baby reluctantly to his nurse, who took him back into the bedroom and put him in his cot. Charity looked about the room, thinking how very Greek it was and how foreign it must have seemed to Faith. A modern, rather flamboyant ikon took pride of place on the wall, showing the sugar-sweet faces of the Virgin and Child looking completely unreal against the beaten gold and silver of their clothing. Before it hung two little red lamps, neither of which was lit. The rest of the furniture was very simple. A well-scrubbed table stood in the centre of the room, around which was arranged four hand-carved chairs. An embroidered cloth had been taken off the table, neatly folded, and placed on a second table that was the only other piece of furniture in the room. On the floor was a violently coloured orange rug, with matted pile probably caused by frequent washing. In the bedroom, Charity had glimpsed only a large double bed and the baby's cot. She thought there might have been a wooden chest at the foot of the bed, for otherwise there was nowhere to keep one's clothes and other possessions that she could see in the whole house.

'What happened to all Faith's – things?' she asked Loukos as they seated themselves at the table.

'I took all the books and papers to my apartment in Athens. The rest of the things were disposed of.' His eyes rested thoughtfully on her shadowed face. 'If I had known you were coming, I would have left her clothes—'

'It doesn't matter!' Charity said hastily.

48

'Your sister had no money of her own,' Loukos went on. 'She owned nothing apart from her husband, so there was no reason for her to make a will, or anything like that.'

Charity smiled. 'I can't imagine her making a will anyway!' she said. 'And if Nikos had given up his business career, I don't suppose he had all that much either! They wouldn't have lived here if he had, would they?'

It was impossible to read Loukos' expression. 'Are you cold?' he asked her courteously. 'The winter is short here, so the houses are built for the long summers, but there is another heater which can be lit.'

'No,' she said, 'I'm quite warm. It's the wind that's cold.'

The Greek woman came back into the room and plonked a bottle of open wine on to the table. Some glasses appeared from nowhere, and she poured out the wine, urging Loukos to taste it to see if it pleased him.

'You have your wish,' he said to Charity. 'This is a resinated wine. I have told Iphigenia to bring some water for you.'

If he had wanted her to drain her glass no matter how the wine tasted, he was successful. It had a harsh taste of pine and she could well understand why some people likened it to varnish. Her first sip repelled her, but by the time she had forced most of the glassful down her throat, she was actually beginning to like it, or at least not to care how it tasted.

'I don't often drink wine,' she remarked carefully.

He grinned, 'I never would have guessed it!' She found herself unable to meet his eyes and curiously breathless, and was distinctly relieved when Iphigenia brought in an enormous, steaming dish of some kind of stew and began to serve them with generous helpings and equally large hunks of coarse bread.

It was a happy meal. Charity was able to forget that Faith had ever had anything to do with the house, it was so unlike anything she had ever known about her, and anyway, the

49

same magic that Loukos had woven about her the evening before came back to her. She felt as though she was on the edge of some great discovery and rather liked the sensation of hovering on the brink, without yet having to take the step that would take her into the future.

When Alexander awoke and began to cry, she was sorry that he had brought the meal to an end. Iphigenia brought him out of the bedroom, newly changed, and settled him on Charity's knee. She asked some question and Loukos translated, 'She asks if you want to feed him?'

'Oh, may I?' said Charity, much pleased. 'He's very small, isn't he?'

'Newborn babies are apt to be! He's only seven weeks old now.'

'I don't know how Faith could bear to leave him!' She went a little white. 'Though I'm glad she did,' she added. 'Poor little mite!'

'She would have done better to have stayed with him,' Loukos retorted curtly. 'Hysterical women are more nuisance than they're worth!'

Charity bit her lip. 'That isn't very kind,' she objected.

'If she had been my wife, I should have known how to deal with her! She would not have gone flying out of my house like that, no matter what I had done. Her place was with Nikos' son, not indulging herself by imagining herself hardly done by and making herself unhappy!'

'So Nikos had done something!' Charity exclaimed.

Loukos shrugged. 'He was her husband, and there was the child. That should have been enough for her!'

Charity shook her head. 'Most English women feel that they have some rights as well as their husbands. Perhaps she was hardly done by. One doesn't necessarily imagine these things!'

'One has no right to happiness, my dear,' Loukos answered. 'Be one man or woman.'

There seemed no answer to that, so Charity busied herself

50

with offering Alexander his bottle, fascinated by the fierce concentration with which he took the teat and sucked at the milk inside. Loukos watched them for a while, but apparently the sight didn't please him for he threw himself back on to his chair and began to drum his fingers on the table in front of him. His hands were seldom still, Charity thought with amusement. He used them constantly when he was talking, to underline a point, or even in a self-expressive gesture that saved having to use words at all. When he was not talking, he was constantly playing with any object that came to hand, as if the different textures were a constant source of delight to him. No wonder the Greeks had been sculptors before all else in the arts!

Half the milk had gone when the braying of the donkey down below told them they had a visitor. Loukos frowned across the room at the door, but made no move to get up to greet whoever had come.

'Iphigenia!' he called out, and jerked his head towards the door. The Greek woman stumbled across the room and opened the door a crack, letting in a gust of cold wind.

'Thespinis Ariadne Vouzas, *kalos orisate!*'

'*Kalos sas vrikame!*' The voice was light and very feminine, as were the footsteps that came hurrying up the stone steps. Charity looked up from feeding Alexander, wondering who this unknown woman could be. She almost sprang into the room, pausing in the entrance and giving them look for look. She had the classic Grecian features and carried herself well, though a certain heaviness of the shoulders gave her the full-breasted, matronly look of a Demeter sadly seeking for her lost daughter, Persephone. When her eyes fell on Charity, she was visibly dismayed.

'You are Faith's sister,' she said abruptly and in English.

Alexander, deprived of his milk by the angle of the bottle, let forth a roar of aggrieved temper, recalling Charity's attention to what she was doing. Charity smiled down at him and made some soothing noises.

'This is Charity,' Loukas said in the calm that followed. 'Ariadne Vouzas, one of our more famous actresses. She was to appear in Nikos' productions next summer.'

Ariadne looked sulky. 'He got me a room in the village,' she explained. She gave Loukos a swift glance from under her eyelashes. 'Loukos didn't approve,' she added. 'I'm going back to Athens to please him, but he is very hard to please. Believe me!'

Charity did. She watched, fascinated, as Ariadne crossed the room and placed both her arms round Loukos' neck in a threatrical gesture that was none the less gracious. 'Say you are pleased to see me!' she begged him.

'Why are you still here?' he countered.

'I thought somebody else might continue with the production of the plays, but nobody will. It is all so miserable without Nikos!'

Loukos leaned forward and kissed her gently on the cheek. 'More miserable still for Alexandros!'

Ariadne shrugged, 'He has his aunt.'

'And you have all that awaits you in Athens,' he answered, smiling. And he kissed her again.

CHAPTER FOUR

CHARITY averted her eyes, wondering at her own outraged feelings. They had probably always been on kissing terms. It was more than possible that their families had known each other for years and years. Besides, Ariadne had been going to work for Nikos and *that* had nothing to do with Loukos. But what was it that awaited her in Athens? A new part? Alexander hiccuped and protested, waving a small fist in the air while his aunt did her best to clean his face with a tissue.

'You look as though you know what you're doing,' Ariadne observed.

'Up to a point,' Charity agreed. 'I have had friends with young babies, but I've never actually had much to do with them myself.'

Ariadne smiled with malicious amusement. 'What a pity Iphigenia won't go to Athens!' She turned to Loukos. 'What are you going to do with him? Your mother isn't going to like having him at Kifisia.'

'There's always Electra,' Loukos said dryly.

Ariadne laughed. 'Ah yes, Electra! I had forgotten her! Poor little Alexandros, I hope she doesn't completely smother him with love!'

Loukos frowned. 'You are frightening Charity by speaking like that!' he rebuked the Greek girl. 'She wants Alexandros for herself.'

'Only Alexandros?'

Loukos shrugged. 'That is no business of yours. Charity, if you haven't finished feeding that baby, Iphigenia will have to do it. If you wish to see the museum, we must hurry. I don't want to be too late delivering Alexandros to my parents.'

Charity gave her small nephew a hug and put down the

finished bottle. 'He has a terrific appetite – another Archer characteristic!'

Loukos let that go by. He took the child from her with competent hands and went himself into the bedroom to put him back into his cot. Ariadne looked sulkily after him.

'I thought you were looking at Delphi this morning? If I'd know you were going back there I wouldn't have come! It depresses me to see that glorious theatre and know that I shall never now play there. We had such wonderful plans, Nikos and I. He was a genius in his way, though I am afraid that your sister never believed it. She was always saying that Eva Sikelianos had done it all before and that it didn't require genius to copy a good idea. Nikos was the first to admit that the American woman really *lived* with the ancient Greeks, and that her production of *Prometheus Bound* was truly fantastic. She made no compromises with the modern ideas about the play. That is where Nikos would have gone one better. He would have made it a wonderful experience also, but a *modern* experience! Faith never appreciated what he was trying to do. She wanted him to go back to Athens.'

Charity looked round the room. 'I'm not surprised,' she said.

'Oh, this? This is not important! She didn't have to come to Arachova—'

Loukos emerged from the bedroom. He said something in Greek which reduced Ariadne to a hurt silence. Loukos went on in English, 'If Nikos came to Arachova, of course Faith would be with him. She was the woman of his house and his wife, Ariadne!'

Charity did her best to cover the awkward silence that followed the rebuke by asking Loukos what had happened to Eva Sikelianos. 'Didn't you say she was buried at Delphi?'

'She died here,' he answered, still sounding ruffled. 'They were giving a feast in her honour, in gratitude for the Delphi

54

festivals that she had made possible. She became unconscious and she was never to recover. They placed a coin between her lips and put a pomegranate in her hand, and
buried her in the graveyard high up above the temple.'

'Oh, how wonderful for her!' Charity exclaimed.

Ariadne gave her a curious look. 'That is what Faith said.
She said again and again that she had entered *Heliou Basi-
leuma* – you know, the Sun Kingdom. How would you say
it?'

'The radiance of Apollo,' Loukos supplied.

Charity jumped. '*Faith* said that?'

Loukos gave her a wry smile. 'She had a thing about
Apollo too,' he said. 'But for different reasons!'

'Oh?' she prompted him, but he only went on smiling.

'Nikos said that Faith knew nothing about him!' Ariadne
broke in sulkily. 'She didn't like Delphi, for instance.'

'Why not?' Charity asked.

To her surprise, Ariadne coloured guiltily. 'She was
afraid,' she muttered. 'There have been earth tremors in the
past, and she was always afraid that the rocks might fall on
her.'

'Not in Delphi,' Loukos said abruptly, 'but here in Arachova. I think it was an excuse to get Nikos to go back to
Athens. She wasn't comfortable here.'

'No,' Charity said, 'I don't suppose she was. Poor
Faith!'

'Come,' Loukos said again. 'We must be going!'

The bitter wind blew her skirts hard against her legs as
Charity made her way down the stepped alley in the wake of
the other two. Ariadne, she noticed, had tucked her hand
firmly into Loukos' arm. Charity had always been brought
up not to hang on anyone's arm and that made her feel all
the sillier as she struggled with the sheer female envy that
gripped her as she saw their heads close together, with Ariadne chattering nineteen to the dozen, her eyes never
leaving Loukos' face. She was being tiresome and rather

55

childish, Charity told herself. The others were old friends, whereas she was an outsider and an unwelcome one at that. What did she care what they did? What did it matter to her?

She almost slipped as they came up level with the car. She didn't hurt herself, but it set her on edge. Ariadne had already ensconced herself in the front seat and she struggled with the back-door handle for what seemed like minutes before she realized that it was locked. She banged on the window, but Ariadne made no move to open it for her. It was Loukos who reached right across the car and unlocked it, his smile warm and friendly and all the more hateful because of it. Let him keep his charm for Ariadne!

The short drive back to Delphi went by in a blur. Ariadne had changed to Greek for her non-stop conversation and Charity couldn't have understood her even had she wanted to. She tried to tell herself that the other girl was being bad-mannered, but she knew better and so the whole argument lacked conviction. Everyone had spoken English in her presence if they could, ever since she had come to Greece, and if Ariadne had been speaking English now she probably wouldn't have been able to hear her above the noise of the engine.

She thought Delphi unbearably beautiful as they came in sight of it again. The wind whipped up the grey-green of the olive trees, moving like some haunted sea at the foot of the shrine. The Phaedriades, the Shining Ones, were less menacing than when she had first seen them, reflecting the gold of the wintry sun that had struggled through the misty clouds for another short interval. It was warmer than it had been in Arachova.

Loukos looked significantly at his watch and then at Charity. 'Half an hour,' he said. 'We can't wait any longer!'

'Half an hour,' she agreed. She wondered if he would come in with her, or whether he would sit in the car with

56

Ariadne, looking down the valley towards Itea, the small port where most pilgrims had always landed, finding it easier to come to Delphi by water than by the long road from Athens.

He got languidly out of the car, stretching his hard, golden-skinned body. 'Do you want me to come with you?' he asked her.

She nodded quickly, unwilling to actually say that she wanted him. 'Do you mind?' she said as they approached the museum steps together.

'I was coming anyway,' he told her. 'I never come here without paying my respects to the Charioteer!' He gave her a mocking look that brought the colour stinging to her face. 'I'm sorry to hurry you through your first visit,' he added, 'but you will come back.'

'Yes,' she said. 'I shall be visiting Alexander as often as I can!'

'I thought we hadn't seen the last of you,' he drawled. 'If you start up the stairs, I will buy the tickets and catch you up, then I can point out to you the most important things you ought to see.'

Had she gone by herself, she would have glanced briefly at every exhibit, giving equal value to each, but Loukos had quite other ideas. He showed her the curious beehive stand at the top of the stairs, that had once held three serpents twisted together, before it had been taken to Constantinople by Constantine where it has long since fallen apart, though it can still be seen. He told her that this had marked Delphi as being the navel, the centre, of the world, and how Zeus had released two eagles, sending them in opposite directions, and it was at Delphi they had met and taken their rest.

He showed her the archaic statues of the two brothers, Cleobis and Biton, whose mother had been a priestess of Hera. One day, when her oxen had failed, they had dragged her carriage all the way to the Temple, and she had prayed

57

for them to receive the greatest thing in the gift of the gods. And her prayer had been answered. They had gone to their rest that night and had never woken again, dying in the full powers of their manly strength.

Charity's eyes had brightened with tears as she had looked at them, thinking of Faith and Loukos' brother, Nikos. Had death been a gift to them? How could one know?

But everything else paled into insignificance as they came into view of the statue of the Charioteer. No illustration had prepared Charity for the reality of this, the dearest treasure of Greece. The young man – he was still but a boy – stood, his hair-line gleaming with sweat from the effort he had just made, his eyes gleaming with triumph, shadowed only by the frail wire eyelashes. His feet were so remarkably fashioned that had they moved, it would have been no surprise. Here was the pinnacle of all art, an object that men flew thousands of miles to Athens and drove all the way to Delphi just to see for themselves, in preference to everything else that the ancient world has to offer. This was perfection. And she, Charity, was standing before him now.

'Anything else is a bit of a comedown after that,' Loukos said roughly as they turned away, 'and I'm afraid we've run out of time.'

'I don't want to see anything else,' Charity said.

Loukos took her arm in a friendly way and she did not draw away from him. It was a moment of pure happiness and she was glad of the contact and hoped that he wouldn't let go until they went back to the car.

'Is Ariadne coming back to Athens with us?' she asked as they went down the stairs.

'I hope so. Be kind to her, Charity, if you can. Her parents are rather displeased with her and it is costing her a lot to go back to Athens.'

'Isn't she old enough to look after herself?' Charity said, trying not to sound as catty as she felt. 'I mean, she is over twenty-one, isn't she?'

Loukos smiled. 'In Greece that matters less than in England – for a woman. Naturally her parents wish to protect her to the best of their ability. That is our way!'

Charity twisted her lips into a smile. 'Didn't they want her to act in Nikos' play? It seems harmless enough to me.'

'Delphi is a long way from Athens,' Loukos answered. He stopped, his hand tightening on her arm. 'Well? Are you going to live up to your name and be kind to her?'

Charity swallowed and nodded. 'If you want me to.' She blinked, wondering why she couldn't be more gracious when it obviously meant such a lot to him. 'I'll try, but I don't think she likes me very much. I don't think she liked Faith either!'

'There were two sides to that!'

'And I'm on Faith's side! *Someone* has to be! Nobody considered her. Look at that house at Arachova. How could she live there? We've never had much, apart from a great hulk of a house in which we froze every winter, but we did at least have a chair to sit on! If you want to know, I think Faith was quite right. Nikos should have gone back to Athens and whatever his business was. He had an obligation to support his wife and child, not play around at being the producer of the ages!'

'Well, well,' said Loukos.

'I don't care what you say,' Charity went on, 'I shall *still* be on Faith's side!'

'Why should my saying anything make any difference?'

Her eyes widened. '*It doesn't!*' she denied. But it did, and why she couldn't have said to save her life. 'She was my sister. . . . Do you think she may be in the radiance of Apollo too?'

'No, you little pagan, I don't! And *don't cry*! If you so much as shed one tear, I shall regret not taking a much firmer line with you, Charity Archer. Faith may have been

59

your sister, but she was married to Nikos, and what went on between them is no business of yours!'

'Whereas you can make anything your business, I suppose?' she snapped. 'Nikos, Faith, little Alexander, even – *even me!*' She took a deep, sobbing breath, now thoroughly wound up. 'Even Ariadne!'

'You certainly seem to intrude into my family's affairs. It will be a relief to both of us when this Colin of yours gets here!' He let her go suddenly, the look he gave her dark and brooding. 'Don't try me too far!' he shot at her. 'I may not have your red hair, but my patience is very easily exhausted!'

'*You* don't like me either!' she declared. Then, feeling remarkably silly for having said such a thing, 'What have I done anyway?'

He laughed suddenly and took her arm again. 'You are,' he said, 'and that's quite enough, believe me!'

'I am?' Could it mean that he saw her as someone in her own right, and not just as Faith's sister? 'What if Colin doesn't come?' she added.

'It doesn't bear thinking about,' he said gravely. He gave her a push towards the car. 'Would you be more comfortable in the front, with the child?'

She shook her head. 'It doesn't matter. I can give him all my attention if I have him in the back, and Ariadne can talk Greek to you!'

'But then it's all Greek to you, isn't it, my dear?' he said.

This was so very nearly the truth that Charity refused to answer but got into the car with her head held high, ignoring as far as she could Ariadne's interested gaze.

'Didn't you like him after all?' the Greek girl questioned her. 'I thought you'd come out swooning with ecstasy, but you look angry instead. I told you he would be a disappointment to you. I find him dull—'

'Who?' Charity asked, and then in complete disbelief:

60

'*Loukos?*'

'The Charioteer.' Ariadne gave her a peculiar look. 'Didn't you see him?'

Charity's face cleared as if by magic. 'Oh, *him*! I liked him better than anything! Better than anything I've ever seen. Better than Michelangelo's David – and that's pretty wonderful!'

Ariadne dismissed this with a slight shrug, turning to smile at Loukos as he got into the car beside her. She said something sharply in Greek and he answered her, looking amused. Charity sat further back in her seat, feeling suddenly tired and defeated. Loukos was right – it was all Greek to her. She would never have believed that Faith would have lived in such a house, but then she hadn't known Nikos. Perhaps he had been worth it all, the cold and the apparent poverty and living in Arachova. And if Faith had loved Nikos enough to put up with all that, what could have happened to make her run away from him?

She gave up the puzzle and gave her attention to the passing countryside. Blue painted, square beehives nestled in groups of a dozen or so in the sheltered dips of the hills. Large stones held them down in the wind that was still blowing across the scrub-covered slopes. Charity wondered what it was like there in summer, when the sky was a piercing blue, and one could stand up above the eagles as they swooped down into the valley in search of their hapless prey. Perhaps one day she would see it like that, a long time from now, when she would know all the answers and would know, without a single doubt, exactly who Charity Archer really was.

Iphigenia came out of one of the colourful shops in Arachova, carrying Alexander. Her face was heavy with grief as she settled the baby on Charity's knee. She put her broad, practical hand on the crown of his head and stroked the bright red down that would one day be hair. Then, with a murmured blessing, she turned and left them, her back sag-

61

ging with the weight of her sorrow at their parting. She never looked round again, but went back inside the shop, leaning over the brazier and warming her hands, while the other women of the village clustered about her.

Charity eased the baby into a more comfortable position in the crook of her arm, her own eyes filling with tears. How she wished she could speak Greek! She could have talked to the Greek woman, someone who had actually known Faith while she had been living in Arachova, and someone whom she was convinced had been fond of her, just as she had been fond of her son.

'Oh, Alexander!' she whispered against the baby's head. Her eyes met Loukos' in the driving mirror and she moved hastily, trying to get outside his vision. Her thoughts at that moment were private thoughts and she resented his ability to read her mind.

'Alexandros will be all right with my parents,' he said. 'While he is so young he won't notice how old they are.'

'Babies need love. Will they love him? Will they?'

Ariadne gave a long, low laugh. 'Electra will supply the love! Electra will suffocate him with love!'

Loukos nodded. 'It is only a temporary arrangement. If my parents find it too much, I shall move Alexandros to my apartment and find someone else to look after him. Electra can manage in the meantime, but she is not very young now herself.'

Charity said nothing. She closed her eyes and tried to think about Colin with some enthusiasm. She had a mental picture of him as she had last seen him and thought gratefully how lucky she was to know him. His gold hair would curl no matter how hard he tried to flatten it with various lotions, but otherwise his appearance was remarkable only for its extreme neatness. He preferred his clothes to be on the conservative side, dark and uncrushed, worn always with a white shirt and a sober tie. His life was similar to his clothing. He worked in a bank and he had a small rented flat that

62

he kept clean and tidy himself, and which Charity had only seen on two brief occasions when he had invited her up for a quick drink. Nobody could possibly disapprove of him, not even Loukos! If she married him, and he too wanted Alexander—

She was surprised to find that they had already gone through Levadia and that they would soon be close to Thebes and back on the motorway for Athens. She wondered if she could have slept and glanced anxiously down at Alexander. He was fast asleep, his cheeks pink with warmth and well-being, and her heart melted within her.

'When does Alexander have his next feed?' she asked Loukos, leaning forward a little to do so.

'When he wakes up. With a little luck, he will sleep the whole way to my parents' house. My mother hates receiving people she hasn't met in the evenings. She has become very stuck in her own ways.'

Charity thought guiltily of the time he had allowed her at Delphi. He turned his head and smiled at her. 'Stop worrying, Charity!'

She felt winded and terribly conscious of the warm texture of his skin and the way his well-formed hands held the wheel. She couldn't take her eyes off him. How dearly she would have liked to touch him; to know if his lips were as firm as they looked, and if the line of his jaw would be hard and strong against her fingertips. With an effort, she tore her eyes away, and tried to control her breathing. Thank goodness it would soon be dark! What was the matter with her? The sooner Colin came the better! She remembered she had not yet asked him to come and decided then and there not to rely on the vagaries of the postal system, but to telephone him that very evening, the moment she got back to her hotel!

The motorway passed quickly. They stopped for a few seconds just outside Athens to pay their dues at the barrier and, a few minutes later, turned off the main road, following the signposts to Athens. Kifisia, now a well-heeled suburb of the city, was full of charming villas and tree-lined avenues. Here and there, the lights of a café spilled out across the road, but most of the light came from the villas themselves, for all the ones that were being lived in in the winter as well as in the summer had their porch lights lit, shining a welcome to the visitor and a warning to the prowler alike.

Loukos drew up outside a small, square villa, set fairly far back from the road and surrounded by its own walled garden. There was no doubt that money had been spent on this dwelling, in complete contrast to the house at Arachova. The garden was beautifully kept, with two fine palm trees that bowed their trunks towards the house as if they were pointing the way to it.

Ariadne peered out of the car window and shivered. 'They will not wish to see me!' she said to Loukos.

He put a hand on her shoulder and pulled her close against him. 'They don't know, and I'm not going to tell them. What would be the point? They have been hurt enough already. Come in, Ariadne, and see them. They will think there is something wrong if you stay out here by yourself.'

Charity looked inquiringly from one to the other of them, but they both ignored her. She wished that they had not spoken to each other in English if they hadn't wanted her to know what it was all about. What on earth was there about Ariadne to upset Loukos' parents? She gave him an impatient look and, holding Alexander closer to her, she darted out of the car, grazing her arm on the side of the door.

'You can put that injury down to your red hair,' Loukos observed. 'Working yourself up into a temper about nothing!'

'It isn't nothing! It's very bad manners to talk at each other like that in front of me! You can keep your secrets—!'

'I shall!' he said, unperturbed. 'Shall I take the baby?'

64

'*No!* He's just waking up and you may frighten him.' She set off for the house without waiting for him, her heels pounding the paved path in her indignation. But she did not get very far before his hands descended on her shoulders and he turned her right round to face him, his eyes black and unreadable despite the light from the porch.

'*I* will take Alexandros, ' he said quietly but inexorably. 'It is time he grew used to me and, Miss Archer, if I do frighten him, it is still nothing to do with you!'

'It is!' she protested. 'A frightened child is everybody's business, and Alexander is my nephew!'

'I have not forgotten, but I think you forget that he is also *my* nephew!'

Reluctantly, she relinquished the baby into his arms, noticing even as she did so the gentle way he supported the infant's head. More annoying was the way that Alexander gurgled up at him, the tears he had been about to spill while he had been in her arms quite forgotten. Charity stretched her cramped arm surreptitiously.

'You don't allow me to forget – *anything*, Kyrie Papandreous!'

To her indignation he laughed. He pulled her hair with his free hand hard enough to hurt and laughed again at her expression of angry discomfiture. 'Shall we call a truce until your fiancé arrives?' he offered, smiling.

Her temper died away at the mention of Colin and she felt peculiarly depressed. 'I want to see as much as I can of Alexander,' she pleaded. 'I can't keep coming to Greece. It's too expensive!'

'We'll talk about that when he comes too.'

'But I prefer to make my own arrangements—'

'As you keep telling me. Colin has my sympathy!'

The unkindness of that made her wince, but she had no time to make a suitable retort, for the front door was opened wide and an elderly woman took one look at the group on the doorstep and uttered a piercing shriek of welcome, swooping down on to the unsuspecting Alexander with great cries of glee.

'Electra,' Ariadne said *sotto voce*.

'My aunt. My mother's sister,' said Loukos.

Charity prepared herself to greet the Greek woman, but Electra had eyes for nobody but the baby. In a few seconds she had torn him away from Loukos and had gone rushing through the house, announcing his arrival to anyone who would listen. Charity looked after her, astonished. She heard Ariadne giggle behind her and remembered how she had said that Electra would supply all the love that Alexander was likely to get in his grandparents' house. Her eyebrows rose and she gave Loukos a look that she hoped was as dignified as it was defiant. If he thought Electra was a suitable person to look after *her* nephew, she did not! The gleam in his eyes made the colour rise in her cheeks and it was she who looked away.

'As I said, a *temporary* arrangement,' Loukos said thoughtfully.

'I should hope so!' said Charity.

It was less of an ordeal than she had expected to meet Loukos' parents. His mother was small and dumpy. She sat on a heavily upholstered chair, her hands constantly busy with the elaborate embroidery that was her hobby and her joy. When Charity was introduced to her, she inclined her head a fraction of an inch and bade her welcome in Greek. She didn't address her directly again, but at intervals Charity could feel her watching her every movement and hoped that she was not comparing her too unfavourably with Faith.

Her husband had a look of his son, but was smaller and had put on a great deal of weight in recent years. His beard was quite white and flowed down over the knot of his tie, which reminded Charity of the statues she had seen of Socrates. She wondered if Kyrie Papandreous was also of a philosophical turn of mind, but she doubted it. He had too

66

much of an eye for beauty, as his obvious delight in Ariadne's company bore witness. He was a long time flirting with her, complimenting her on her appearance and squeezing her hands with his. Then, quite suddenly, he turned to Charity.

'So you are Faith's sister?' he said in Greek. Ariadne translated the assertion for him, giving Charity a quick grin of sympathy. Charity only nodded. 'Why do you come now to Athens? We began to wonder if your sister really had a family in England! It is too late for you to come now. She and Nikos are dead.'

'I didn't know that when I came,' Charity said steadily.

The old man stood up and went over to the mantelpiece, searching among the clutter of small statues and ikons propped up against the wall. He came back with a photograph in his hand which he threw down on to Charity's knee. 'My son, Nikos.'

Charity looked at the likeness, her fingers trembling. Had this really been Faith's husband? This strange, untidy young man, with his brooding eyes and his look of having seen everything there was to see. She noticed that he held a glass in his hand and wondered if the photograph had been taken when he had perhaps been overdrinking.

'I'm sorry,' she said aloud, not knowing what else to say. Ariadne snatched the photograph away from her and returned it to the mantelpiece.

'Nikos was – how do you say it? – something else! He was more alive than anyone else I know! This photograph says nothing about him, *nothing*! How could it? How can a camera know what a man thinks and feels. Not even Spiro and Xenia, his own parents, understood how it was with Nikos!'

Loukos stopped talking to his mother and looked across the room at Ariadne. 'Nikos was not difficult to understand. He had a wife and a child and was interested in the theatre. It hardly adds up to very much to make such a mystery

67

about, does it?'

Ariadne gaped at him, but she finally shook her head in agreement and sat down quickly near to Xenia Papandreous, who smiled at her and began to show her her embroidery.

Only Spiro Papandreous remained unsatisfied. 'There was more to Nikos—' he began in heavily accented Greek.

Loukos put his arm about his father, embracing him unselfconsciously. 'Charity thinks I look like Apollo. I have already told her that Nikos looked far more like Dionysius! Don't you agree?'

The old man thought about it, his eyes snapping with amusement. 'Yes, that is the truth,' he said. 'I must be Zeus himself to have produced such sons!' And he laughed. 'Apollo and Dionysius! It is good. It is very good!'

CHAPTER FIVE

LOUKOS was right about the hotel restaurant, just as he was right about so many other things. The food was a failed compromise between Greek and English menus in an attempt to please everybody. It did not please Charity, but she ate there more often than not because she didn't like to go into the *tavernas* by herself, to be stared at and discussed by every male in the place. It made her feel like a race-horse in the ring, and she longed for Colin to come if only to protect her from their admiring comments and the personal remarks that flew about her head whenever she went out.

He had said he would come. He had even agreed that it was well worth the expense of her telephoning him if they could be together over Christmas.

'I didn't like to think of you going so far by yourself,' he had told her over the crackling wire that was the best the operator could manage so near to Christmas, 'even when you were going to your sister. Why don't you come home?'

'Because of Alexander!'

'Oh yes, the baby.' There had been a long pause. 'Then I'd better see if I can get a flight out tomorrow.'

'Oh, darling, that would be marvellous! It may – it may be a bit expensive. Can I help?'

'It will have to be my Christmas present to you,' Colin had said.

Charity had known a peculiar prickling sensation at the back of her neck. She couldn't ever remember exchanging presents with Colin before.

'Oh yes?'

'Well, I'm not coming out to see a stranger, Charity! We'll do the thing properly. I'm *glad* you telephoned, though it must be costing you a pretty penny?'

'It is,' she had murmured weakly.

'Never mind, love, I'll be there in person tomorrow. What's the name of your hotel? Book me a room there, will you?'

She had told him the name of the hotel, unaccountably relieved that he seemed to expect to have a room to himself. For a moment she had wondered— But she might have known that Colin was not like that. He was the most solid, respectable person that she knew. He would believe in marriage and all the old virtues as naturally as other people breathed air. It would be good to see him again. She knew where she was with him. He would never confuse her, as Loukos confused her, constantly reminding her that she was a woman and that therefore her opinions were of no account, and yet making her glad that she was a woman, more glad than she could say. Colin saw her as a person, a responsible person, as capable as he was to look after herself. *He* would never want to make her decisions for her! Surely that was something to admire him for?

When he did come, all she felt was a disappointing lack of excitement. She had gone early into dinner, hoping to escape to her room before she was waylaid by some other English tourist in the bar. It was not that she disliked talking to her compatriots, but she had found herself strangely reluctant to tell anyone what she was doing in Greece and, as they were only too willing to tell her every detail of all they had seen in Corinth, or in the shops in the Plaka, she had felt that she was doing less than her stuff by keeping a defensive silence about her own affairs. Anyway, she looked up to thank the waiter for filling her glass with the delicious cold water that one never has to ask for anywhere in Greece, and at that moment Colin had walked into the dining-room, looking tired and out of temper.

'Colin!' she exclaimed.

He saw her then and came over to her table, throwing himself into the chair at right angles to hers. 'I never thought Athens would be like this!' he exclaimed.

'Like what?'

'Oh, I don't know. I caught a glimpse of the Acropolis coming along. It's rather disappointing, don't you think? It's smaller than I'd imagined, and the rest of Athens didn't look anything much!'

Charity swallowed. 'It's quite a modern city,' she said.

'With ancient trimmings? Have you been to look at them yet?'

She shook her head. 'Not yet.' She took a deep breath, willing him to share the glory of this particular piece of information: 'I've been to Delphi!'

'Good for you!' he said. 'More ruins?'

She nodded, bereft of words. She sought for some change of subject, feeling somehow responsible for his disappointment in the city she had brought him to. 'It was nice of you to come,' she said.

'It wasn't particularly convenient.' He studied her face with a faint smile. 'To tell the truth, I hadn't realized we'd quite reached this point of our relationship. Obviously absence makes the heart grow fonder as far as you're concerned! It does mean what I think it means, doesn't it?'

'I suppose so.'

Colin stopped smiling. 'What does that mean?'

'I don't know,' she confessed. 'Oh, Colin, I know I ought to be able to tell you exactly how I feel, but I only feel numb – except as far as Alexander is concerned! He's an adorable baby! And he's the only piece of Faith I have left.'

'That doesn't seem much loss,' Colin said frankly. 'You haven't seen her for years, and you didn't have much in common with her when you did see her.'

'Colin!'

He muttered an apology. 'But you must admit it's true all the same! I know it was a shock to you to find Faith had been killed, but you aren't usually maudlin about that sort of thing—'

71

'What sort of thing?' Charity demanded, feeling cold and hurt.

'Well, you took your father's death pretty well,' he pointed out. 'It isn't like you to rave about some baby you know nothing about!'

'He's my *nephew*!'

Colin accepted the menu from the waiter and waved it in the air. It was a pedantic rather than a forceful gesture, quite different from the clever way in which Loukos used his hands to make a point. 'Good lord, Charity, I have half a dozen nephews and nieces, and I don't care a row of beans for any of them! I mean, I send them a few bob at Christmas time — that sort of thing, but I don't go on about them! They're not *my* children. I daresay I'll feel differently about my own. Well, one does, doesn't one?'

'Does one?' Charity retorted. 'I couldn't say, never having had any!'

Colin actually grinned at her. 'That's probably what you need! You wouldn't carry on about Alexander then.'

'I am not carrying on about anything!' Charity informed him slowly and clearly, so that the whole dining-room could hear her.

'Ssh!' he begged her. 'People are looking at you!'

'I don't care if they are!'

Colin looked grimly at her. 'I don't think being in Greece has improved you. You'd never have called attention to yourself in this way in London!'

'I never needed to! Oh, Colin, please don't let's quarrel! I know you don't understand why I should feel like I do about Alexander, but you will when I tell you all about it. He's so alone, poor little mite. The Papandreous family hated Faith, so what sort of life can he look forward to? There's Loukos, of course, but I'm sure he doesn't really care. None of them do, not like I do!'

'Who's Loukos?' Colin asked.

'Faith's brother-in-law, and you should have seen the

house where Faith had been living in Arachova! I'm not surprised she wanted to run away, though that was awful too—'

'I thought you said she'd been killed near Delphi?' said Colin, who liked to get things straight.

'It's a village just beside Delphi,' Charity explained patiently.

'Not that I know where Delphi is,' Colin went on, 'but I can always look it up on a map. What made Faith go off the road?'

'I don't know,' Charity said. 'Nikos was killed too. I suppose they were both driving too fast.' She blinked. 'Loukos says that being thrown off the cliffs of Parnassus was the punishment for sacrilege against the shrine. It made me think of that terrible piece by Euripides. I haven't been able to get it out of my mind ever since. "*Seize her! Throw her from Parnassus, send her bounding down the cliff-ledges, let the crags comb out her dainty hair!*"'

'Good God!' said Colin. 'Serve you right for reading such stuff!'

Charity looked at him with affection. 'Oh, Colin, it is good to see you! You're so – so *normal*! And you will ask Loukos if we can have Alexander, won't you?'

Colin's face took on a pink shine of pleasure. 'I've always thought you were pretty normal too,' he said. 'I expect all this has been a shock to you.'

'You see,' Charity said, doggedly pursuing her point, 'Loukos won't even *talk* to me about Alexander. He has a very old-fashioned idea about women—'

'Thinks they're only good for the one thing?' Colin suggested with a grin.

Charity coloured, remembering that she had had some pretty extraordinary ideas herself about Loukos. It hadn't occurred to her to wonder what it would be like to feel Colin's lips on hers, but then she thought she knew. She looked at him critically across the table and wondered why

73

it should irritate her that he should look so pale, and that his mouth should seem to her to be tense more than firm. It wasn't his fault that he worked in London and not in the warm sunshine of the Aegean.

'Well?' said Colin. 'I gather he tried it on with you?'

'Of course not!' Charity denied, shocked. 'It's only that he feels that women should be protected. You know, that their men should look after them – that sort of thing! He practically thinks that a woman *belongs* to her husband!' she added indignantly.

'And it matters what he thinks? Who exactly is Loukos?' Colin inquired.

'Loukos Papandreous. He's Nikos' brother.'

Colin gave her a jaunty smile, looking relieved. 'He stands as close to Alexander as you do, then? Doesn't he want the child? If his ideas about women are as peculiar as you say they are, I should have thought he'd think it his duty to bring up his brother's child? Same name, and all that. Why should you be saddled with the infant?'

'But that's just it! He says I can't have Alexander because he's Greek like his father and has to be brought up in Greece. But Faith wanted him to be English! She wanted *me* to have him!'

'Have you told Loukos that?' Colin asked sharply.

'Of course I have! But he won't even discuss it with *me*. He says he'll talk to you about it—'

Colin laughed. 'Cheer up, Charity! He'd have to talk to me about it anyway if I'm going to marry you. He'd have to safeguard the child. I might not want him, or refuse to support him—'

'You wouldn't?' Charity exclaimed, going white.

'Of course not, silly! Not that I do want him much. But I want you enough to put up with him, I dare say.'

Charity was touched by his honesty. 'And you will talk to Loukos?' she prompted him.

'I don't see why not,' Colin said. He blew out his cheeks

74

and patted his stomach with an important air. 'He'll have a hard time getting the better of me! It's an English speciality, sorting out the Greeks, starting with Lord Byron and going right up through the last war. Greece is part of the Balkans, you know. They've never been able to work anything out by themselves.'

Charity's jaw dropped. She reminded herself that Colin hadn't yet met Loukos, but even so, she had never thought of him as *insular* before. He seemed like a stranger, far more foreign than – some people who really were foreigners. Some people? *Loukos!* She caught herself up hastily, more than a little put out at the way her thoughts were going. Anxiously she forced a smile and burst into speech: 'Quite right! He's bound to give way if you talk to him.'

Colin merely nodded and went on eating his food. Charity wished she had not stooped to trying to flatter him. Trying to? She had flattered him! She stared across the table at him. How odd it was. She had never flattered Loukos, despite his views on her sex, so why should she feel obliged to butter up Colin when he was the one who believed in women thinking and doing for themselves?

'It was nice of you to come,' she said again. 'Was it terribly expensive? I – I booked you a room here. It's on a different floor from mine, but it has a better view. You can see right across Athens, and the lights, and everything!'

'Sounds a bit noisy,' Colin commented.

'Oh, Colin!'

'Sorry,' he said. 'I'm tired, that's the trouble. Though, as it's really only six o'clock now, I ought to be full of beans. It's probably the strain of flying and all that.'

Charity, who had thoroughly enjoyed her own flight only a few days before, agreed that it was very tiring and that perhaps he had better have an early night, while she let Loukos know that he had arrived and would like to see him. 'Will any time do?' she added. 'He may be working most of

75

the day.'

Colin shrugged his shoulders amiably. 'As long as it isn't in the middle of the night! I loathe the way foreigners turn the night into day. I like to get off to sleep at a proper hour.'

Charity sighed. 'I'll do my best,' she promised. 'I'll go and phone him now.'

'Okay, sweetheart. I'll order something for you at the bar and then we can go on up. What will you have? Your usual sherry?'

Charity had already nodded when she suddenly rebelled against any drink that was considered her usual anything. If she hadn't disliked the aniseed flavour of ouzo so much, she would have asked for that. Instead she asked for the next best thing. 'I'll have some retsina. I'm getting to quite like it.'

'Isn't that resinated wine? I'm told it tastes disgusting!'

'Why don't you try some?' Charity suggested, but Colin was appalled by the very idea.

'I'll stick to whisky,' he said. 'Safer.'

Charity picked up her handbag. She wished earnestly that she didn't have red hair and that she had a better control over her volatile temper. 'It'll cost you,' she warned him.

'It'll be worth it,' he said dourly. 'I'll put it against the economy I'll make by your drinking the native stuff and it won't seem so bad!'

Charity's eyes flashed, but she said nothing. She hurried up the stairs to the reception desk and stood for a long time looking at the notices that had been stuck up on one of the walls in the entrance lobby, giving details of the various tours that were available to the hotel's guests.

'Can I help you, madame?' one of the young men behind the desk asked her.

'Yes. I want to make a telephone call. Can you get the number for me? I want to speak to Kyrios Loukos Pap-andreous, but if anyone else answers, I don't speak

76

Greek.'

'Of course, madame. Have you the number?'

She searched in her handbag and drew out Loukos' card, giving it to the man. 'Thank you very much,' she said.

Loukos himself answered the phone. Charity put the receiver to her ear and felt a wave of relief sweep through her at the sound of his voice. 'It's me,' she said. 'Ch-Charity.'

'*Pos isthe*, Charity?'

'Wh-what?'

'I asked you how you are? Do you always stammer on the telephone?'

'No, of course not. Only I was a bit nervous of having to speak to someone else. I mean, you might have been out, or there might have been someone else there?'

'If you are asking me if I am alone, no, I am not,' he said in an amused tone of voice. 'I have Alexandros here – and Electra. It was not a success leaving him with my parents. His crying disturbed my mother—'

'But he doesn't cry! He didn't cry on the journey from Delphi, not once!'

'Perhaps he prefers your touch to Electra's! Well, Charity, and how can I help you? Have you grown bored with your own society?'

Charity ignored that. 'Colin is here.'

'Ah!' The long-drawn-out syllable was full of significance and Charity grew more hot and bothered than she was already. She had a feeling that Loukos wasn't going to like Colin and she wanted, quite passionately and for some obscure reason that she wasn't prepared to question, that he would admire her taste in men, and even if he were to like Colin, there was nothing much to admire in him, and she was beginning to wish that there was no reason for the two men to ever meet.

'He wants Alexander as much as I do!' she went on.

'That I take leave to doubt,' Loukos answered. He still sounded amused, almost as if he knew the state of nervous

77

anticipation she had worked herself into. 'When are you bringing him to see me?'

'Can you manage tomorrow?'

'Of course. Shall we say half past two? My office is closed until four o'clock for lunch. Oh, and Charity, you will leave your young man alone with me, is that understood? You can talk to Electra and Alexandros in the other room.'

'Oh, but Colin—'

'I will see him alone,' Loukos repeated. 'This has nothing to do with Alexandros. We have first to decide that he stands some chance of making you a good husband, and that will be easier for us both if you are not present.'

'But you can't!' Charity gasped. 'Colin wouldn't understand! Loukos, it's nothing to do with you!'

'I think Colin will understand very well. I am beginning to think it is you who are not very sure of him.'

Charity stared miserably at the receiver in her hand. How could he do this to her? Colin was bound to be rude to him and then he would *never* allow them to have Alexander. Loukos wasn't the sort of man one was rude to twice!

'Of course I'm sure of him!' she claimed, sounding pitifully unsure even to her own ears. 'We'll *both* be there at half past two.'

'Very well, I will see you then. Good night, Charity.' The amusement in his voice became very marked. 'I am glad you are no longer unprotected, and there is nothing to stop me from stealing a kiss from you. Will you be glad too?'

Her outrage was clearly audible, but unfortunately not very deeply felt. Long after she had replaced the receiver, she felt a warm glow of excitement that he might make good his threat. It didn't mean anything! Everyone had moments when they would like to be kissed by someone they didn't care twopence about, just because they had a skin the colour of olive wood and eyes as bright as the sun. If Apollo called, who had ever resisted him?

Colin was yawning into his drink when she joined him in

78

the bar. 'This whisky cost me almost a pound!' he complained. 'Well, have you fixed it up with this Greek fellow for us to see him?'

Charity nodded. She considered for a wild moment telling him that Loukos was planning to vet him as to his suitability as a husband for herself, but her courage failed her at the look on his face. Another man would have roared with laughter, as in other circumstances, she would have done herself. But then, she thought with a touch of despair, Colin never had had any sense of humour. And at that moment she disliked him very much indeed!

Loukos' apartment was in a stylish block on the Vasileos Konstantinou, not far from the Royal Palace. A little way up the road was the American Embassy and the Hilton Hotel. In the opposite direction was the Athens Stadium, too small for modern events, but nevertheless the place where the first of the modern Olympic Games had been staged. The buildings were almost all made of the same Pentelic marble from which the Acropolis had been rebuilt twenty-four hundred years before. It was evidently a very fashionable part of Athens and, Charity suspected, an expensive one. She cast a sidelong glance at Colin as they entered the shadowed entrance and were whisked upwards in the silent lift.

'A man of substance,' Colin remarked with appreciation. 'His credit standing must be pretty good – I wouldn't mind living in a place like this!'

'Perhaps the company he works for owns it,' Charity suggested. 'I don't think the Papandreous family is particularly wealthy – not by Greek standards. The house in Arachova was barely furnished, so Nikos couldn't have had much apart from what he earned.'

Colin gave the carved ceiling on the landing a respectful look. Charity wished irritably that he would take that awed look off his face before Loukos saw him, but Colin seemed dwarfed by his surroundings and quite determined to behave like a nervous schoolboy on an unexpected treat from school.

Loukos opened the door to them himself. 'Hullo, Charity. As you can hear, our nephew is screeching his own inimitable welcome!'

Charity laughed before she could prevent herself. The baby's cry was not really very loud, but then neither was he very old.

'This is Colin Anderson,' she said awkwardly. 'Colin, Loukos Papandreous.'

Colin lifted his hand in a vague signal of greeting, ignoring Loukos' outstretched hand. She saw Loukos lift an eyebrow. It couldn't have been worse, she thought. But she was wrong. In his hurry to get through the door, Colin pushed her to one side, his enthusiasm alight for a picture of the Houses of Parliament he had spied in the hall over Loukos' shoulder.

'The first civilized thing I've seen in Athens!' he said warmly. He turned his head, patently adding up the probable cost of the furniture. 'Very nice!' he approved. 'Funny thing, Charity gave me quite the wrong impression of you.'

Loukos's expression was inscrutable. 'Did she though? I am afraid she has had an unsettling few days since she came to Athens and is rather emotional just at the moment in her judgments.'

Charity interrupted indignantly, 'I didn't say anything about you at all! Except that you won't let me have Alexander—'

Loukos suddenly grinned, his eyes sweeping over her red hair. 'Did you tell Colin what I wanted to see him about?' he asked. He might as well have thrown cold water in her face. Her eyes widened guiltily.

'Oh, please don't!'

'But I shall!' He put his arm round her and hugged her to him. 'Electra is waiting for you in her own room at the end

80

of the corridor. You can rejoin us for coffee when we've had our chat. Okay?'

The touch of his hand on her back set her heart pounding. She would have argued with him further, anything to put off the humiliation of having him interview Colin like a Victorian father – when he wasn't her father, or *anything* to her! – but her mouth was dry and her knees were trembling, and she couldn't bring herself to meet the brilliance of his eyes.

'Okay,' she said.

Colin was only too willing to be taken into the sitting-room. Charity was just able to catch a glimpse of his pale face glowing with pleasure as Loukos said something to him. But then Loukos firmly shut the door behind them, shutting her out of their masculine conference. She stood there for a long moment, sure that her whole future was about to crumble about her ears. *She didn't trust Colin!* The knowledge came like a thunderbolt, reverberating round her mind. Loukos would make mincemeat of him and she wouldn't be there to give him a push in the right direction, and Loukos had planned it that way. But why should he care whom she married? The answer was only too painfully clear. He didn't. He was merely exercising the traditional Greek care of the orphan and the unprotected female.

She stumbled along the corridor and knocked on Electra's door, hoping against hope that Electra spoke a few words of English. The Greek woman had Alexander on her knee and she eyed Charity suspiciously as she entered the room.

'Why do you come here? You want to take the baby away from me, is that it? But Loukos has promised that I shall look after him until he can make a proper home for him. That's all I ask, a few weeks with a baby to look after! Must you take that away from me?'

Charity was startled into compassion. 'I only want to see him,' she said. 'I won't take him away from you. You see, I love him too!'

Electra's straight back sagged with evident relief. 'He has so little love,' she said in muffled tones. 'A baby needs much love!' She rocked Alexander back and forth, beginning to smile. With her black hair falling out of the knot at the nape of her neck, and the deep lines cut into her face between her nose and mouth, she yet had a maternal look about her that had never been allowed to flower before. 'Who is that man who came with you?' she asked.

'Colin? He's a friend of mine. I – may marry him.'

'If Loukos approves?'

Charity frowned. 'It has nothing to do with Loukos! Only I haven't entirely made up my mind—'

To her indignation, Electra laughed. She had the same full-blooded laugh as Loukos, enjoying her mirth with every bit of her, only in her case it was because jokes were too few and far between not to make the most of them. 'Of course it has to do with Loukos! Your father is dead, no? And you have no brothers to arrange the settlement with your intended. Loukos says you have as little as your sister before you, so he will not be marrying you for your money.'

Charity's cheeks burned. She sat down on the vacant chair beside Electra and put an absent hand out to the baby, who clasped her finger in one fat hand and gurgled back at her. 'Faith didn't do very well out of her marriage,' she observed.

Electra's black eyes snapped with some remembered emotion that Charity could only guess at. 'What did she expect? A runaway marriage is always difficult for the families to accept. How can they know anything about the bride? We accepted Nikos' word that the girl was chaste, but she herself would tell us nothing! Xenia despaired of ever making anything of her. It was uncertain even that she loved Nikos, but then it is difficult to tell with the English. Are you in love with this man of yours?'

'I think so,' Charity murmured.

Electra leaned forward, intent on what she was about to

say. 'Xenia is not an easy woman, even though she is my sister. I could understand why Faith did not confide in her.' Her voice dropped almost to a whisper. 'The baby disturbed her and Loukos had to bring us here to his own apartment. I didn't want to come at first.'

'Why not?' Charity asked, annoyed to find herself whispering too.

'Ariadne! Loukos thinks I don't know about her, but me, I see more than he thinks! I know her family are hardly speaking to her – and how glad they were when Nikos took her out of Athens to be in his play at Delphi. And I know why! Did you know that she was promised to be married?' Electra nodded her head several times. 'Now he will have nothing to do with her, as one would expect! She is ruined! I was afraid that if I came here, she would be here too.'

'Here?'

'She is in love with Loukos. Why else did she allow him to do this terrible thing to her? Who will marry her now? She may have thought that Loukos would, but why should he marry her now? I thought the affair was still going on.' She lowered her eyelids virtuously. 'Ariadne's parents are personal friends of mine. I could not turn a blind eye to their daughter's bad behaviour, so I had rather not be here. But Loukos says she will not be coming here while the baby and I are here. It is better so.' She nodded again, her eyes on the baby's face, not expecting any answer from Charity.

How could she have missed it? Charity wondered. How could she not have seen it? And she shivered, quite suddenly ice-cold.

CHAPTER SIX

'WELL, what did he *say*?' Charity had become increasingly cross as she and Colin had walked back to their hotel, and as Colin had maintained a smug silence over what had passed between the two men. 'He must have said something!'

'Yes, he did, but not about Alexander—'

'About me?' Charity demanded, with a tightening about the lips. Less and less did she want Loukos to poke his nose into her affairs. He had Ariadne – surely she was enough for him! Wasn't it enough that he had ruined the Greek girl's life, without getting excited about Colin marrying a girl he knew nothing about, and who wouldn't thank him for his interest at the best of times?

'In a way,' Colin admitted. 'I don't know what you've been telling him about your life in England, Charity, but I don't think you should have made out that you were lonely exactly. After all, I was about, wasn't I?'

'Of course you were!' Charity agreed warmly.

'Well then, why make out you had to do everything on your own?'

'I don't think I did,' Charity answered. 'I wouldn't say such a thing even if it were true—'

'I know you had a tough time with your father,' Colin went on, not listening to her at all. 'Still, you wouldn't have thanked me if I had made all the arrangements for you, would you? This Papandreous fellow seems to think that I should have taken on the whole lot, told you what to do and seen that you did it too! I tried to tell him that we weren't on those sort of terms at the time—'

'We aren't now!' Charity interrupted.

'No,' Colin agreed.

'I'm not helpless!' Charity went on. 'Really – the Greeks

have the oddest ideas about women! But I'm nobody's —
thing, to be bossed about merely to make some man feel
good!'

'Quite right!' Colin approved. 'You're too practical yourself, much more practical than I am. That's why I'm asking
you to play along with Loukos Papandreous. If you play
your cards right, I think he may make some sort of marriage
settlement on you. He seems to feel some kind of responsibility for you, because of Faith, I suppose. She married his brother, so he considers you family. It could be a
good thing for you.'

'Nonsense!' Charity scoffed. 'Nikos was as poor as a
church mouse!'

'But Loukos isn't!' Colin pointed out.

'No, but I wouldn't accept any of his beastly money even
if he offered it to me. He may be thinking of settling something on Alexander, but that would be different. *We*
couldn't use any of it!'

Colin looked thoughtful. 'He didn't say anything about
Alexander. It was you we were talking about. He had the
nerve to ask how much I'm earning!'

Charity coloured. She bit her lip, torn between embar-
rassment and an odd sense of gratitude to Loukos that he
should go to so much trouble on her behalf. *Lucky Ariadne!*
Even if he wasn't going to marry her! She gave a little gasp
at her own thoughts and tried to meet Colin's look of astonishment.

'Are you *laughing*? It wasn't at all funny, let me tell you!
He didn't think I was earning enough to keep myself going
and that I had no business to be considering marriage at all!'

'Goodness!' said Charity.

'Of course I told him it was all your idea,' Colin said
airily. 'I'd have preferred to wait a bit—'

'And you told him that?'

He nodded. 'I told him that you wouldn't wait because of
Alexander.'

'Oh, thank you very much! It doesn't sound as though you want to marry me at all! You don't have to, Colin. I can manage very nicely without you—'

'Not if you want Alexander!'

She blinked. 'Yes,' she admitted, 'I do want Alexander. But having him wouldn't be enough for you, would it?'

'He won't come empty-handed,' Colin said dryly.

Charity looked at him, seeking some sign of the love she thought he had for her. 'Do you – do you mean me?' she asked him.

He grinned. 'I suppose I do,' he agreed.

It wasn't very loverlike, she thought. She would have liked it better if he had swept her up into his arms and kissed her until she forgot all about Alexander, all about *everything* in the joy of being loved by him. But that wasn't Colin's way. She had to remember that he had his own way of doing things, and that he would never kiss her like that. It had its advantages, of course, and she would do better to dwell on them. He would never, for example, use his superior strength to win an argument with her. He would expect her to argue the toss on its merits. And he would apply the same standard to her. He would despise her if she used her sex to cajole him into agreeing with her – if he knew that that was what she was doing. She knew already she could flatter him in a way that Loukos would have seen at once, and would have laughed straight out of court. But she refused to think about Loukos – she would not!

'Colin, you did tell him that our marriage has nothing to do with him, didn't you?'

He looked startled at the urgency in her voice. 'But I keep telling you, Charity, that he's determined to make himself in some way responsible for you. If he likes to make some cash settlement on you when we get married, why should we refuse him? Money never does any harm!'

'I won't discuss it!' Charity retorted. 'He's nothing to me, even if his brother did marry my sister! Any money we need, we can make ourselves by our own efforts. I can work too, Colin. I won't be a drag on you!'

'I know, darling. But you'll never earn more than a pittance at best. Loukos was talking about real money.'

'I won't accept a penny from him!'

Colin laughed. 'I haven't your scruples. I'll accept every penny I can get. I made it pretty clear that I don't expect to lose by having Alexander either. He was pretty close about how we'd stand as far as the baby is concerned, though. I asked if Nikos had left anything for the education of his son, but he just looked at me in that way he has, as though he can look right into one's mind and doesn't much care for what he sees. Jolly uncomfortable sensation, I can tell you! I thought if I kept quiet for long enough he'd be bound to say something, but he didn't. Just let the silence drag on until I said a great deal more than I meant to. I even told him that I'd had to borrow the cash to fly out to Athens for Christmas!'

Charity knew now that she had never known anything about humiliation until that moment. She had thought she did. But that was before Loukos had come into her life, turned her emotions and her most dearly held theories upside down merely by looking at her out of those dark, brilliant eyes of his, and now he had brought her to this nadir of mortification by exposing Colin's tepid feelings for her, not only to his remorseless gaze, but also to her own.

'I told you I'd pay your expenses!' she managed to say.

'But if he's prepared to pay—'

'*Never!* I'll pay every penny of it myself!'

Colin shrugged, puzzled in the face of her wild anger. 'Why didn't you speak to him yourself if you don't approve of anything I said?'

'Because he wouldn't discuss it with *me*! He's a Greek, after all!'

'You sound as though you admire him for it!' Colin said resentfully. 'If I tried to exclude you—'

'I don't!' Charity denied in a shaken voice. 'I think, if

anything, I hate him! Oh, what does it matter? He can't buy us with his horrid money, and when he realizes that, he'll leave us alone! There'll only be Alexander, and surely any arrangements we make about him can be done through our solicitors?'

'That'll cost a pretty penny—'

'I don't care what it costs! I don't want to have anything more to do with Loukos Papandreous, and that's that!'

'You'll have to,' Colin said. 'He's asked us to go to his place for Christmas Day and I said we would.'

'Oh, Colin, I don't want to go!'

'Why not? He should do us pretty well. He has the where-withal to make it quite a day!'

'I prefer to share Christmas with the people I love,' Charity said. She tried to throw off the despair that had gripped her ever since she had been forced to realize that Colin was envious of Loukos' wealth. How could he be? She didn't think that Loukos could be half as rich as Colin seemed to imagine, but even if he were, it didn't matter to them. It was none of their business, just as it was none of Loukos' business to start arranging marriage settlements on her behalf!

'I've said we'll go,' Colin repeated with a sulky droop to his mouth. 'As a matter of fact I'm looking forward to it. It's the first decent thing that's happened since I got here.'

'All right,' Charity agreed abruptly, 'we'll go!'

She parted from Colin in the hotel foyer, going straight up to her room in the lift. She badly needed time by herself to sort herself out. What was she to do? One thing was certain, it had been a mistake to ask Colin to come to Athens. She hadn't doubted at the time that she wanted to marry him, it hadn't seemed particularly important whom she had married as long as it meant that Loukos would allow her to have Alexander. But she wasn't at all sure now that she wanted to marry Colin. She hadn't liked the way he had looked round Loukos' apartment, calculating the cost of everything just like an adding machine. And to think that he would accept a marriage settlement from Loukos, as if he needed some bribe to go to the altar with her! Yet, if she didn't marry him, she knew Loukos would never let her have Alexander. She would see him for a brief fortnight every second year, because she wouldn't be able to afford to come to Greece more often than that. She would lose him entirely, and with him her last link with Faith.

About Loukos himself, she resolutely determined not to think at all. It was only too easy to dwell on the image of him that seemed to have taken up residence in her mind. The bright brilliance of his dark eyes, the way his gleaming black hair grew out of his scalp, the hardness of his golden-skinned body, the touch of his essentially masculine hands that could coerce or be as gentle as a woman's, and most of all the firm moulding of his face and the longing she felt to feel his lips against her. But there, peering at her over his shoulder, was Ariadne, who had known him more intimately than she ever would. It wasn't pleasant to know that that fact in itself could make her feel quite sick with jealousy. But when she tried to tell herself that Loukos would expect of any woman something that she was quite unprepared to give to any man, an unquestioning deference in every sphere of life, she only longed the more for him to ask it of her.

Christmas Eve came and went. Charity tried to put her problems behind her and join in the general merrymaking in the hotel, but the thought of the morrow reduced her to such a pitch of nerves that even Colin noticed she was not herself and advised her in a rather heavy-handed manner to have an early night and not to follow her earlier intention of going to Midnight Mass.

Then Christmas was upon her and there was no longer any escape from seeing Loukos again. Surprisingly, it was Colin who held back as the lift doors opened and it was left to Charity to ring the bell and to be the first to greet Electra as she opened the door to them.

89

Charity had decided that it would be enough for her to take a bottle of Scotch whisky with her, and some sweets for the women, who probably didn't drink whisky. She handed both packages over to Electra in the hall, accepting in return Alexander from her hands, who gave her a long, searching look and finally fell asleep with the ease of the very young.

'If he would have slept a minute ago how happy I would have been!' Electra sighed. 'He is having wind all morning!'

'Poor mite!' said Charity. She smiled at her nephew's peaceful face and was suddenly aware that Loukos had joined them in the hall and was watching them. The colour flew to her face and she would have given anything to have taken to her heels and run. 'Happy Christmas!' she murmured, forcing herself to stand her ground.

'Happy Christmas,' he returned gravely. 'Are you going to put Alexandros to bed, or do you wish to nurse him for a while?'

Her eyes flew from Alexander to Colin's disapproving face and back again. She couldn't bring herself to look at Loukos at all. 'I'd like to hold him for a few minutes. He needs loving—'

'Then bring him into the sitting-room. My parents are already here and are waiting for you to arrive to have a drink.' He smiled directly at Charity. 'Is the whisky a hint that that is what you prefer? Or will you have retsina?'

'Retsina,' she said shyly. 'I'm acquiring a taste for it.'

When they had all sorted themselves out, Colin was the only one who was drinking whisky. He had the bottle close beside him, pouring it out for himself. Charity hoped that he wouldn't take it as an invitation to help himself to more than a couple of drinks, or think it amusing to celebrate Christmas as noisily as they had in the hotel bar the night before.

Xenia Papandreous looked at the picture that she and Alexander made with something like approval. She patted the seat beside her on the sofa and beckoned imperiously to her sister to translate for her.

'You are fond of the child and he feels that,' she said. 'We are all too old to have our lives turned upside down by him – even Electra, who will make herself ridiculous over any baby! I have been telling Loukos that you must have Alexandros with you, once you are married, of course.' She turned bodily in her seat, the better to survey the unsuspecting Colin. 'You are to marry him?'

Charity bit her lip and nodded. 'It isn't completely sure yet.' She despised herself for being so indefinite! Why couldn't she commit herself and have done? Why did she always have to say maybe, and I think so, instead of a resounding yes?

Xenia actually smiled. 'It is better for people to marry their own kind,' she said. 'That was the mistake your sister made. I am sure you will be very happy with your Englishman.'

Electra looked rather less sure as she obediently translated her sister's words. She hesitated for a long moment, her mouth working anxiously. 'The baby is Greek. He will be cold and unloved with your Englishman!'

'He'll have me!' Charity said evenly.

Loukos came and stood behind her, his hand on Electra's arm. 'There is no question of Alexandros going to England. The child will remain with me. Charity already knows that!'

'But when I'm married—' Charity protested.

Loukos touched the baby's cheek with a very gentle finger. 'I have decided that Alexandros will stay in Greece whether you marry or not. His place is here with me. There is no point in discussing it further.'

Electra made a small, joyful noise in her throat. 'Shall I take him and put him down in his cot? It will soon be time for lunch.'

Loukos nodded. He picked the baby up himself, without looking at Charity, and handed him over to Electra. Charity looked down at her hands, trying hard not to cry. What was the use of *anything* if she couldn't have Alexander? She felt Loukos' hand hard on her shoulder and attempted a smile.

'I have a small Christmas present for you,' he said. 'I would like you to have it before lunch.'

'For me?' She gulped, afraid of giving way completely before the interested eyes of the Papandreous family. 'I d-don't think I want anything from you,' she stammered.

His eyebrows rose, but he said nothing. Charity immediately felt she had been ungracious and flushed. 'I m-meant that the only thing I want is Alexander!' she rushed on. 'L-Loukos, your mother is quite right. There's no place for a small baby here.'

'If you want Alexandros you will have to make up your mind to staying in Greece,' he answered.

'But I can't!'

'Then you'd better make the best of things as they are,' he advised, quite gently, indeed almost as though he sympathized with her dilemma. He took her hand in his and pulled her up on to her feet, leading her across the room to where the table was already set for lunch.

'You shouldn't give me anything,' she began helplessly. 'You don't have to! I'm nothing to you—'

'It is something quite small,' he cut her off, smiling. 'You can say, if you prefer it, that it is not from me at all. It is a gift from Apollo.'

Her eyes widened. 'What do you mean?'

'This,' he said. He took a small box out of his pocket and opened it, drawing out a small gold brooch shaped like a laurel leaf. 'The Badge of Apollo!'

She said nothing at all, but stared at the brooch almost as if she was afraid of it. He pinned it to the front of her dress, a smile lifting the corners of his mouth, as though he knew— But he couldn't know! She didn't *know* herself, so how could he know! A rising wave of panic swept through her and she took a swift step backwards, wrenching the brooch out of his hands, closing the clasp herself with fingers that shook no matter how hard she tried to control them.

'It's beautiful!' she whispered.

He really smiled then. 'Aren't you going to thank me?' he asked her.

She glanced across the room towards the others, but none of them were showing any interest in the exchange between herself and Loukos. 'You, or Apollo?' she asked.

'Perhaps it is the same thing,' he said, his expression inscrutable. He followed her quick look across the room in Colin's direction and took her hands in his. 'You have your protector with you to object – if he wishes to do so,' he went on. 'So why should you not thank me? Do you want me to think you ungrateful? Or that you don't like the brooch? Or – that Apollo no longer has any sway over you?'

She said the first thing that came into her head. 'He didn't answer my request at Delphi.'

'I told you you might get a double-edged answer that you might not like, but you have to be patient. What do you expect? A miracle?'

'It would only be a very small one.'

He looked amused. 'I think you will have your answer sooner than you think,' he told her. He pulled her close against him, putting one hand on the nape of her neck beneath her hair. His eyes blazed and she gulped, bracing herself for what was to follow. She must treat it as lightly as he did! A casual kiss, a graceful murmur of gratitude for the brooch, and then she could return to Colin's side and forget all about it.

Only it wasn't like that at all. He was very gentle. He kissed her eyes, and both her cheeks, and then, finally, her mouth. She thought her heart had stopped, but then it rocketed against her ribs, beating out a message that she didn't want to succumb to and was even more afraid that he might hear.

'Isn't that enough gratitude for—?'

93

His lips came down on hers again and it was much better than she had imagined it might be. She had no defences against the wonder of it. She shut her eyes and kissed him back, only to find herself put away from him and having to support herself. She held on to the wall, not daring to look at him, until her shaking knees felt a little less like rhubarb. Then, at last, she smiled vaguely in his direction and said, 'That was for Apollo!'

He didn't look much as though he believed her. 'Tell that to Colin!' he grinned at her. He led her by the hand back to the others, offering her a seat right beside Colin, who was busy explaining the English taxation system to Electra. The Greek woman, who had never filled in a form in her whole life, having always been protected from such hazards by one or other of the male members of her family, looking stunned and at a complete loss. Charity gave Colin a furious glance and rushed into speech herself, horrified to hear herself asking Electra, Xenia, and even Spiro, the most personal questions about the way they lived and how they usually celebrated Christmas. And all the time she was conscious of Loukos' amused expression as he watched her making a fool of herself. But the funny thing was that none of them seemed to mind what she asked them. They were only too ready to tell her all about their most personal affairs, and even more ready to ask her about hers.

'Was your father a wealthy man?' Spiro demanded suddenly, his curiosity getting the better of him. 'We have often wondered about Faith's family.'

Charity shook her head. 'I don't think there has ever been a rich Archer,' she said. She wondered at the quick look Loukos exchanged with his father but she had no means of knowing what it meant, so she dismissed it from her mind. She turned to Colin, dismayed by his glare of sulky disapproval, and smiled at him. 'Money doesn't mean much to us, does it?' she encouraged him.

'Only the lack of it,' he joked. The sound of his voice

94

jarred on Charity and she bit her lip. What was she going to do if she couldn't bear even to listen to Colin talking? She had never minded what he said before. She had even thought him rather clever, the way he understood all about stocks and shares and could talk about money matters with the most knowledgeable, using his banking flair to the best possible advantage. So why should she quibble now whenever he opened his mouth?

The Papandreous family had done their best to produce a typically English Christmas dinner. They had been unable to buy a plum pudding in Athens, but the turkey was everything that could be desired, served with chestnut stuffing, roast potatoes and brussels sprouts. Charity wondered if they would have eaten something similar anyway, but she didn't like to ask – not even Electra, who had done most of the cooking in between looking after Alexander.

When the turkey had been cleared away, they ate the little honey cakes that the Greeks love so much, and laughed a good deal at the stories Loukos told them in a mixture of English and Greek of the perils of the transport industry, where ships made an incredible amount of money, but occasionally ran aground, or lost their papers in impossible ungetatable places, and aeroplanes made still more money if properly used, but where the knife-edge between triumph and disaster was even more acute. Charity warmed a little towards Colin when he made some intelligent remarks about costing and the difficulties of changing over to new methods of loading and all that that implied for the new freight ports of the future.

Nevertheless, it was a relief when it was at last time for her and Colin to be going. Charity was gratified when both Xenia and Electra clasped her in their arms, kissing her warmly on both cheeks, just as though she really were one of the family and not just Faith's sister, but she was terrified lest Loukos should claim the same privilege and extended a hand to him before he could take any liberties. He took her

95

hand in both his and raised it mockingly to his lips.

'There were no complaints, were there?' he asked.

She blinked, pulling her hand away as if his touch burned her. 'Why should there be?' she returned. 'It meant nothing. We all knew that!'

He lifted an eyebrow, looking very sure of himself. 'The gods are more jealous than Englishmen. Remember that when you wear your brooch!'

Charity felt as though an electric charge had gone right through her. She preferred not to dwell on what he might mean by that extraordinary remark, preferring to take sanctuary behind Colin's rather prolonged farewells, giving a smiling assent to everything he said. She thought though that she would never forget the very masculine way that Loukos eyed her manoeuvres, right up to the moment when the lift wafted her away from his view. He had no right to look at her like that. No right at all! She might have kissed him to thank him for the brooch, but that was no reason to study her as if he had some right to an – *intimate* was the only word she could think of, yes, intimate knowledge of both her mind and her body. Why, he had looked at her as though he owned her!

She shot out of the lift and into the cold, windy street. It was Loukos she was angry with, but it was Colin who walked by her side and who came in for the backlash of her indignation.

'Didn't you mind his giving me the brooch?' she demanded, tossing her red hair back over her shoulders.

'Why should I? It looks a nice piece,' Colin replied.

Charity came to a full stop. All the disappointment she had felt in him all day came to a head. If she could have brought herself to touch him, she would have hit out at him.

'Is that all you can say? That it's a valuable piece? Is that all you care about? Well, it isn't enough! He made me kiss him too!'

96

Your special introduction to the Mills & Boon Reader Service.
A chance to enjoy 4 spellbindin
Romances absolutely FREE.

Four exciting Mills & Boon Romances have been specially selecte
for you to enjoy FREE and without any obligation. You can meet Caroli
her imminent marriage threatened by a misunderstanding . . . Karen,
forced to meet the husband she still loves two years after their divorce .
Sabrina, tragically blinded and fighting a little too hard to be independe
. . . Ravena, about to marry a forbidding stranger to protect her belove
guardian from a terrible secret.

Intriguing relationships . . . memorable characters . . . exciting
locations . . . Our readers tell us that the books we select have them
'hooked' from the very first page. And they're a joy to read to the last
loving embrace.

The Unwilling Bride
by Violet Winspear
Ravena loved her guardian and
desperately wanted to protect him fro
terrible secret about his son. But that
meant marrying forbidding Mark di
Curzio in order to bear him
a son.

The Marriage of Caroline Lindsay
by Margaret Rome
Caroline agreed to marry Domenico Vicari to
give her sister's abandoned baby a home and
security. But Domenico believed the
baby to be Caroline's own.

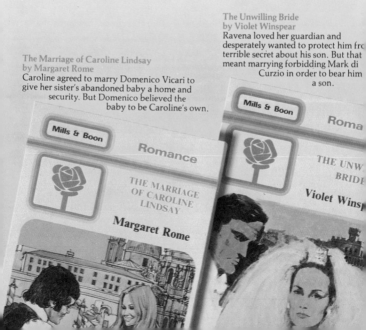

Mills & Boon
Romance

THE MARRIAGE OF CAROLINE LINDSAY

Margaret Rome

Mills & Boon
Roma

THE UNW
BRIDE

Violet Winsp

With the help of the Mills & Boon Reader Service you could receive the very latest Mills & Boon titles hot from the presses each month. And you can enjoy many other exclusive advantages:

No commitment. You receive books for only as long as you want.

No hidden extra charges. Postage and packing is free.

Friendly, personal attention from Reader Service Editor, Susan Welland. Why not ring her now on 01-689 6846 if you have any queries?

FREE monthly newsletter crammed with knitting patterns, recipes, competitions, bargain book offers, and exclusive special offers for you, your home and your friends.

THE FOUR FREE BOOKS ARE OUR SPECIAL GIFT TO YOU. THEY ARE YOURS TO KEEP WITHOUT ANY OBLIGATION TO BUY FURTHER BOOKS.

You have nothing to lose—and a whole world of romance to gain. Just fill in and post the coupon today.

Mills & Boon Reader Service,
P.O. Box 236, Croydon, Surrey CR9 9EL.

Ivory Cane
Janet Dailey
Sabrina coped bravely with the tragedy of being blinded in an accident. But how could she cope with a man who offered pity when she needed his love?

Seen by Candlelight
by Anne Mather
Even two years after their divorce, Karen still loved her husband Paul. To protect her sister from the advances of Paul's married brother Karen must meet him again—a meeting she dreaded.

Mills & Boon Romance

THE IVORY CANE
Janet Dailey

Mills & Boon Romance

SEEN BY CANDLELIGHT
Anne Mather

See overleaf for your FREE BOOKS order form.

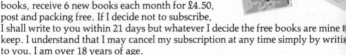

'Why not?' Colin said easily. 'We were all there in the same room. It didn't mean anything. All the people here go round embracing each other all the time, the men as well as the women. Besides, you didn't mind, did you?'

'Yes, I did!' she stormed. 'I minded very much! If you'd been anything of a man you would have called him to account for kissing me. I belong to you, don't I?'

Colin's startled expression would have made her laugh at another time. 'I say, steady on,' he said. 'We may be thinking of getting married, but I hadn't thought of your belonging to me exactly. If you ask me, you're making a great fuss about nothing.'

'I'm not! He was expecting you to protect me from him – and I was too!'

'Then you're in for another disappointment,' Colin told her, refusing to get annoyed. 'I was rather glad he wanted to kiss you, actually. It makes our position a bit stronger. It's no good getting all het up, Charity. *I'm* not going to quarrel with you, whatever you throw at me. I know you well enough by now to know that it's your hair talking and not the real you. And if you take my advice, you'll go on playing Loukos Papandreous along, just as you have been doing. From what his aunt was telling me, he has an eye for a pretty girl and is generous with it—'

Charity stared at him, her anger so great that she was speechless. She swallowed the lump in her throat, her disillusionment so great that she felt she could taste it. She forced herself to walk slowly forward along the pavement, not caring any longer if the passers-by did see that she was crying.

'Colin, you don't love me at all, do you?'

He shrugged. 'Oh, I don't know,' he said. 'I always knew I'd marry you in the end, I suppose. I hadn't thought it would be quite so soon, but that was before Alexander came into our lives. I don't much care to start our married life with a ready-made baby that has nothing to do with me. I think I'm owed something for being prepared to take him on, and I think, if we play our cards right, Loukos will see things my way. Did you hear him at lunch, talking about the ships he owns? That man must be loaded! Oh no, Charity my girl, you're not going to quarrel with me, and you're not going to quarrel with Loukos Papandreous either. If he wants to kiss you now and then, that's okay by me. As long as he comes across with a marriage settlement, he can do as he pleases for the short time we'll be here.'

Charity broke into a run. 'Well, it isn't all right by me!' she shouted at him over her shoulder. 'I don't have to marry you! He won't give me Alexander whether I do or not – he said so! And I don't want to marry you. *I hate you!*'

But Colin only laughed. 'You'll marry me,' he said certainly. 'He doesn't want Alexander, that's for sure, but he won't let you have him without a husband to be a father to the child. You'll marry me, Charity Archer, because I know how to make him give up Alexander—'

'*You?*' she cried scornfully. 'You think you can get the better of Loukos?'

Colin nodded. 'I know I can,' he said.

CHAPTER SEVEN

PERHAPS it was celebrating Christmas abroad that had upset her, Charity told herself. There had to be some reason why she felt at odds with herself and everyone else at the same time. It had been four days since she had seen Loukos and yet she was no closer to getting him out of her mind than she had been on Christmas evening. Why had he had to kiss her in the first place? She had been doing fine until then. He had been Alexander's uncle, a foreigner, a man who had held an attraction for her, it was true, but not this commanding figure who made her feel like a puppet ready to respond to his lightest touch on the strings.

She tried to think about Colin and found that really she preferred not to think about him at all. She had *always* liked Colin, as had her father, but at the moment all she felt was an increasing impatience with him. Poor man, he could hardly open his mouth without her jumping down his throat! And yet the last thing she wanted to do was to antagonize him, because he was the only passport she held to the control of Alexander. He had said he could outwit Loukos and get Alexander for her, and she had no reason not to believe him. She would marry him, of course she would marry him, and then everything would be well and she would wonder why this madness had taken her in Athens making her hesitant and miserable and quite unlike herself.

For the last four days she had hardly seen anything of Colin, which had been partly by her own choice, but must have been partly by his as well, and had seen nothing of the Papandreous family at all. It was only then that she realized how lonely she was. She even went down to the bar to look for Colin and felt a surge of gladness when she saw him there, drinking his inevitable whisky.

'Hullo, stranger,' she greeted him lightly.

He frowned up at her, making no effort to get up. 'I've been here,' he said. 'I didn't think you wanted to see me, skulking up there in your room by yourself!'

She flushed. 'Not skulking!' she objected. 'I've been trying to make up my mind about things—'

'I thought you already had!'

She sat down opposite him, regarding him thoughtfully. 'Oh?'

'You made up your mind, my dear, when you asked me out here to help you. That was your moment of decision.' He smiled, but she felt more uncomfortable than warmed by it. 'Mine was to come to your rescue. What's more, I don't think we shall have any difficulty in getting our way. It would be better if you would play along with Loukos, though. I don't want him getting suspicious.'

'Why should he be?' she demanded.

Colin smiled again. 'It's better that you don't know too much. Just agree with everything he proposes and leave the rest to me!'

Charity shivered, suddenly cold. 'But, Colin, I'm afraid—'

'Oh, heavens! I know he turns you on, but you wouldn't like to live the rest of your life with him, would you? A few kisses won't matter in the long run. You'll have Alexander to console you – think about that!'

'And you?' she said.

'When we get back to London, I'll cling to you both like a leech, my pet. I know when I'm on to a good thing!'

'You mean you love me?' Charity asked, determined to get that at least quite straight in her mind.

'Haven't I always? Relax, Charity, you haven't a thing to worry about any longer—'

'But I do worry!'

He gave her an impatient look. 'I've told you there's no

need! All you have to do is to leave everything to me. That's simple enough, isn't it?'

'It would be if I loved you,' she said slowly. 'I'm not sure that I do. I feel so muddled about everything. You'll have to be patient with me. In England I thought I loved you, but everything was different then.'

Colin laughed. 'It isn't half as important as you imagine,' he said. 'That sort of love doesn't last long anyway. You'll find we'll settle down together quite happily. There's nothing like a little money to help oil the wheels, and we'll have that if I have my way.'

She was so chilled by this bleak view of life that she didn't think to ask him where the money was coming from. She began to wish that she hadn't come downstairs to find Colin. She didn't like the cold way he looked at her, and she didn't like the way his lips thinned almost to nothing whenever he smiled at her.

When the barman came over to her and said she was wanted on the telephone, she knew such a sense of relief that she was afraid. Surely she couldn't want to get away from Colin as much as that?

To make it all much, much worse, when she heard Loukos' voice on the wire her heart turned right over and, if he had been physically present, nothing would have prevented her from walking straight into his arms. As it was, she stood by the telephone in a shattered silence, trying not to sound as desperate as she felt.

'I rang up to thank you for having us for Christmas,' she said abruptly. 'I got Electra.'

'I know,' he said. 'Electra told me. That is one reason why I am phoning now. I have been away these last few days, but now I have returned to Athens and am at your disposal to show you something of my city. Would you like that?'

Charity took a deep breath. 'Yes,' she said.

'Just yes?'

'What do you want me to say?' she countered.

'You could say that you missed me and that you can't wait to see me again.' This was so close to the truth that, apart from a slight gasp that could have been of annoyance, but which she knew was caused by a fluttery warm excitement that she had no business to be feeling at all, she kept a breathless silence and hoped that he would take that as sufficient encouragement to go on. He did. 'Have you been to Sounion yet?'

'S-Sounion?'

'I'll pick you up at the Tower of the Winds at half past two. Bring your watchdog with you and then I can tell you to your face that your nephew has inherited more than your red hair, he has a few of your ways as well.'

Charity swallowed. 'I don't know if Colin will want to come.'

'He'll come,' Loukos said with unexpected certainty.

'I don't know—' Charity began.

'Tell him you're afraid to be alone with me,' Loukos said calmly. 'That won't offend your conscience, because it is true.'

Charity didn't like to say that she had already told Colin something along those lines – and much good it had done her. 'How – how do you know?' she asked.

He laughed. 'I'll tell you this afternoon,' he said, and with that she had to be content.

Fortunately, Colin seemed to be only too willing to go to Sounion. 'It's important that he thinks we haven't anything else to do but have him show us round,' he muttered. 'You especially have got to be *available*, Charity. I don't think you'll find it a difficult part to play,' he added dryly.

Charity didn't care what he thought. She went with him into the restaurant, but she didn't taste a single mouthful of what she ate. She changed her mind half a dozen times as to what she should wear. She even thought of consulting Colin about the problem, but he had his own problems to worry at, and she didn't like to interrupt his thoughts. In the end she

wore a pale green pair of trousers with a turtlenecked
jumper of exactly the same colour. She thought she looked
rather nice, but Colin said nothing when he saw her except
that if she didn't hurry up they would be late.

At Charity's behest, they walked to the Tower of the
Winds. She was glad to find that they had arrived first,
because the sight of the Tower brought back an overwhelm-
ing memory of the first time she had seen Loukos, walking
like Apollo towards her. Colin thought the ancient clock
rather a boring edifice and said so, loud and long. Charity
first tried to defend the beauty of the carvings that depicted
the eight winds, and then relapsed into a huffy silence when
Colin could barely bring himself to look at them.

She didn't notice Loukos at first and wondered how long
he had been standing by the side of the road, leaning over
the rails that rose sharply by the side of the Roman *agora*
and looking down at her.

'Hullo!' she called up to him.

He raised a hand to her and began to walk down the street
to the entrance of the *agora.* 'Are you ready to go?' he
asked.

She nodded, suddenly shy of him. She looked over her
shoulder for Colin and saw him coming slowly over the
rough ground towards them. His walk was stooped and he
looked thin and rather ineffectual. Charity longed to tell
him to hold his head up, but of course she couldn't do that
and so she frowned at him instead.

'I have the car at the top of the steps over there,' Loukos
went on, pointing up the slope behind him. 'Go ahead, Charity, and get in. It is cold out here and that coat of yours is
not very thick. I'll wait for Colin.'

There were more steps than Charity had expected. She
hurried up them, not looking back because she didn't want
to see how Colin would greet Loukos. She didn't want to
feel ashamed of him any more, and she did feel ashamed of
him because he was so ungracious to all the Greeks – not

that Loukos couldn't have put him in his place if he wanted to do so. Panting a little from the exertion of running up the steps, Charity got into the back of the car, leaving the front seat free for Colin. He would expect it of her, of course, for he always said that a man's legs were too long for the back seat of any car, but that wasn't entirely why she had left it for him. That was because she wanted to have the opportunity of comparing the two men without them knowing what she was doing. It was an odd form of masochism, Charity told herself, because she already knew that any life and vigour Colin possessed was drained away by Loukos' greater attractions.

The men got into the front seats without looking at her. Colin was laughing a little, but his expression was cold. 'This is good of you, Mr. Papandreous,' he was saying. 'Charity hasn't wanted to do much sightseeing. I don't think she cares for Greece much, but she ought to see as much of it as she can before going back to England, don't you think?'

'She has time,' Loukos answered.

Colin laughed again. 'I can't spare her for long!' he protested.

'No? But she will be coming to Greece often enough to see Alexandros. I have been meaning to speak to you about this. Naturally, we shall see that her fare is paid whenever she comes.'

'That's good of you, but I don't think it will be necessary,' Colin said. 'If you won't let her have the child, I think a clean break will be the best for us all. Charity gets upset easily.'

Loukos glanced briefly in Colin's direction. 'Then it is up to us to upset her as little as possible. We will discuss this some other time.'

Charity jumped. If only she trusted Colin, she wouldn't mind leaving it all to him, but she wasn't sure that he wanted Alexander, she wasn't sure of anything about him!

'I want to be there when you discuss it,' she announced from the back.

'I think not,' Loukos said quietly.

'But why not?' she protested.

He smiled at her in the driving mirror, completely at his ease. 'Colin will speak for you. We can discuss the matter more freely if you are not there. You must see that, Charity. How can Colin say what he wants himself, if he knows that you want something different and will think him disloyal if he voices his own doubts?'

'But he *does* want what I want!' she exclaimed.

'Then you have no need to worry,' Loukos returned.

There was no arguing with him! Charity turned impulsively to Colin, but her first words died away before she had spoken them when she saw the amused, almost gleeful expression on his face.

'Are you going to agree to my being excluded?' she demanded hotly.

'If that's the Greek way of doing things I don't see why we should object. You don't make things very easy for me, Charity. It will be all right!'

She blinked, well aware of Loukos' sardonic sideways look at them both. She couldn't think why Colin was so confident of getting his own way. She knew now that in the end they would have to do exactly as Loukos decided, and so, if she felt angry with anyone, the logical object of her wrath should have been the Greek, but it wasn't. She felt an anger against Colin who was so *smug*, and sure of himself, and half-baked when compared with Loukos!

Loukos took the main road out to the Apollo coast road that hugged the many bays that the Athenians swam in and picnicked beside in the long, hot days of summer, and which had made Sounion into a pleasant afternoon's ride. Charity maintained a defiant silence the whole way through the pleasant suburbs of Ellinikon, Glyfada, and Voula. She couldn't share Colin's interest when Loukos pointed out the house that had belonged to Aristotle Onassis, and the rather larger one next door that was owned by his sister. She could only despise his interest in people he didn't know merely because they were rich. Had he always been like that? She couldn't remember, no matter how hard she tried to recall the things he had said and done in England. She sighed, no longer able to put off the realization that she had never known Colin well, and that she didn't much like what she did know.

Her eyes were caught by Loukos' in the driving mirror and she blushed, sure that he had read her thoughts. She was even more sure when he said: 'If a woman commits herself to a man, she should trust him to look after her and protect her interests. In Greece, we look very carefully at the man before we allow him to marry a woman of our family.'

'In England we choose our own husbands!' she said firmly.

He shrugged his shoulders. 'I would not allow it. A woman can never see a man as another man sees him—'

'Perhaps we don't want to!'

He looked her straight in the eyes for a long moment. 'So? It seems a cold kind of loving to me. My woman will commit herself to me absolutely, not this half-hearted way of thinking that she may be better off making her own way after all. What future is there without trust?'

'And if the man is untrustworthy?' Charity burst out.

'It is better to find that out before any commitment is made,' he said dryly. 'As I'm sure Colin will agree?'

'We know each other better in England,' Colin said, feeling he was expected to say something. 'I've known Charity for years!'

Charity opened her mouth to contradict him, but, in a way, it was true. They had first met, was it five years ago? But it didn't mean that she knew him any better than she knew – Loukos!

'So you said before,' Loukos drawled. 'Her father approved you as a suitor for her hand. It's nice for her to know that she has you to protect her.'

Colin coloured guiltily. He cast a quick look of appeal over his shoulder at Charity who stared at him, wondering what other claims he had made for himself. She forced a smile, but she was badly shaken by this new slant on Colin's character. Was that why Loukos had let the information drop, because he hadn't believed Colin? Oh, how she wished it was the other way about and it were Loukos who was looking after her interests! She wouldn't have minded then being treated as though she were an incompetent female with no idea of which way she was looking!

They saw the Temple of Poseidon from a great way off. It stood on the summit of the headland, a few crumbling pillars, pale in the winter sunshine, but somehow magnificent. It was fitting that Poseidon's temple should appear to dominate the surrounding sea, as he had been the god of the sea, and it did in a strange way seem to be more a part of the water that lapped the shore below the cliffs than of the land on which it was built.

The wind struck cold as they left the car. Charity shivered, then wished she hadn't, for Loukos was watching her and nothing much escaped him. She tossed her head in the air and set off at a great pace up the slope towards the temple. The men followed more slowly, Colin slouched in his coat, looking miserable, and Loukos with his hands in his pockets, his long legs covering the ground with an ease that Charity could only envy.

'I suppose you know the story of Theseus?' he asked Charity as they gained the temple walls.

She turned and looked at him. 'Tell it to me,' she commanded.

The brightness of his eyes made her turn away, but she was still listening. She thought that she had heard the story once, but it sounded different told by him, just as though he had known the hero himself, and had known him well.

'Theseus was the son of Aegeus, king of Athens, or so some people say. He lived at the time when the Cretans demanded seven youths and seven maidens as an annual tribute to the Minotaur. Theseus volunteered to go with them, to his father's sorrow. He decked the ships with black sails as a sign of mourning and departed. His father had told him that he would be watching every day for the return of the ships and, that if Theseus were slain by the Minotaur the sails would stay black, but if Theseus succeeded in killing the monster, the sails would be white.

'Theseus was fortunate in Crete to catch the eye of Ariadne, the daughter of Minos the king. She gave him a ball of string that he could pay out as he went into the Labyrinth, and which would help him to find his way out after he had killed the Minotaur. All she asked in return was to return to Athens as his wife. Of course Theseus slew the monster and claimed his bride, but on the way back to Athens they passed the island of Naxos, where Dionysius, the god, saw Ariadne and wanted her for himself, so Theseus was forced to leave her there.

'Such was his sorrow that he forgot to change the sails, and Aegeus, standing on this very spot, saw the black sails coming over the horizon and cast himself into the sea below, thus giving his name to the sea where he died.'

Charity plucked a piece of grass and rubbed it between her fingers. 'Couldn't Theseus withstand Dionysius?' she asked huskily.

'He was not sufficiently the hero to take on one of the gods,' Loukos answered, his eyes on her face. 'Ariadne seemed to approve the change in lover. Dionysius was an untidy-looking god, but he knew how to make her happy.'

Charity bit her lip. 'But he was the wrong god for Ariadne!'

Loukos burst out laughing. 'She didn't share your predilection for Apollo!'

'But your Ariadne does,' she observed before she could

108

stop herself.

His eyes glowed and she blushed guiltily. '*My* Ariadne?' he repeated.

'You know very well what I mean,' she said. She hurried up the steps into the temple itself, looking for Colin. She saw him walking away from the temple to the restaurant below. She wished he had said he was going for she would have gone with him rather than to be left on her own with Loukos.

'The floor is very uneven, isn't it?' she said when Loukos joined her in the temple.

'The local villagers thought that this was the ruins of a princess's palace,' he told her. 'They used to come here by moonlight and dig for the gold that they thought she had buried under the floor.'

Charity made a face. 'The columns look a bit battered too,' she remarked. 'Look at all the names that have been carved into them!'

'Some very famous names,' Loukos smiled. He pointed at the column beside him to one name, darker than the surrounding ones because so many people had traced the letters with their bare fingers. It ready simply BYRON, and was surrounded by a host of other inscriptions, many of them English.

> '*Place me on Sunium's marbled steep,*
> *Where nothing, save the waves and I,*
> *May hear our mutual murmurs sweep*'

Charity quoted, slightly surprised that she was able to. Byron had never been a great favourite of hers. Loukos peered at the name, standing so close to her that she could feel his breath on her cheek. She made to move away from him, but he caught her wrist in his hand and pulled her back against him.

'What was all this about Ariadne?' he asked her.

'N-nothing.'

His grasp tightened about her wrist. 'Ariadne is not mine,' he said. 'You shouldn't listen to gossip, *pedhi*. If you want to know anything about me, you have only to ask. But ask me, not my aunt!'

'I didn't ask Electra!' Charity denied.

'But she told you something. What was it?'

'I'm not going to tell you,' Charity stormed. 'It isn't any of my business what you or she does or doesn't do. I'm not in the least bit interested!'

'Indeed?' he said grimly. 'I suppose Electra told you that I was in Naplion these last few days, and that Ariadne was with me?'

Charity shook her head. Was that where he had been? She felt a great weight on her spirit and wished that he hadn't seen fit to tell her about it. 'No, she didn't,' she said.

'We owe Ariadne something as a family,' he went on. 'But that does not make her mine. Understand?'

Charity understood only too well. Hadn't Electra said that he would never marry Ariadne? Why should he? He had already had all he wanted from her. She tore her arm out of his grasp and walked quickly over to the far side of the temple, staring down at the sea below.

'Come here, Charity,' he commanded her.

She hesitated. She glanced at him nervously over her shoulder and stumbled at the bright look in his eyes. 'Why?' she said.

'Come here and you'll find out!' There was a tremor of laughter in his voice that somehow reassured her. She walked slowly back to him, her head held high.

'Loukos, I know you don't like Colin, but you won't let that make any difference—' She broke off, alarmed by his smile. 'You said you wouldn't touch me. You said you wouldn't!'

'While you were alone and had no one to protect you,' he reminded her. 'But now you have Colin—'

'He's gone to the café!'

'Leaving you to me,' Loukos agreed. 'Just as I hoped he would!'

Afterwards, she was to remember that she had made no move to prevent him from taking her into his arms. He had touched her on the shoulders and the panic within her had melted into ecstasy. She had shut her eyes and given herself up to his kiss as eagerly as if she had been in love with him! And he had held her closer still, parting her lips beneath his own, and exploring the curves of her body with his hands. When he put her away from him, she stumbled and would have fallen if he hadn't kept his hand below her elbow.

'Will you tell Colin?' he asked her.

'Why should I? It meant nothing!'

He pulled her back into his arms and kissed her again, not gently as he had before, but as if he wanted to show her once and for all who was master. She thought her ribs would crack and her mouth felt bruised beneath his.

'Please, Loukos, you're hurting me!' she sobbed.

'Nothing?' he repeated. 'Was that nothing?'

She shook her head, wiping away her tears with the back of her hand. 'Why should I hurt Colin by telling him?' she demanded.

He put a hand under her chin, forcing her to look at him. 'He should look after you better. What good is such a man to you?'

'He's k-kind,' she stammered. 'And he looks on me as a person, not just a – a *thing* to kiss whenever he feels like it!'

'Will that be enough for you?' The contempt in his voice hit her on the raw and she winced away from him, hurrying away from him down the slope to the café and Colin. His long legs made it easy for him to keep up with her no matter how fast she went, and she was bitterly conscious of his broad frame just behind her shoulder and of the slight smile of amusement on his face. 'Do you catch fire for him, *ylikia*? Or is it only for Apollo that you forget to be cool and

English, with your independent ideas?'

She was determined not to answer him. She would not! 'Leave me alone!' she pleaded with him. 'Why should it matter to you what I do?'

'You want Alexandros,' he reminded her.

She came to a full stop. 'Yes,' she agreed, 'I want Alexander.' She gave him a helpless look. 'When are you going to decide about him? You must see that he would be better off with me. You must! Your parents are too old to bring up a baby, no matter how much you want him to be Greek!'

'True,' he drawled. 'But will he be better off with Colin? He is not my idea of a lover, allowing you to flirt with other men, and even to be kissed by them!'

She gasped with an exasperated anger that had something to do with her own feeling of disappointment that Colin hadn't stayed by the temple, that he hadn't been the one to kiss her and light a burning fire of desire within her.

'What I do is my own affair!' she exclaimed.

He raised his eyebrows, deliberately mocking her. 'It's as well you have chosen Colin, then,' he said. 'You would not say such a thing to me!'

Charity swallowed, tearing her eyes away from the brightness of his. She turned her back on him and went into the café, looking for Colin. He had found a table near the back of the inner room and he didn't even look up when she sat down beside him and poured herself out a cup of tea from his pot.

'Why did you leave me with Loukos?' she asked him.

'I didn't think you'd mind,' he answered. 'In fact I thought you'd probably enjoy it. You seem to enjoy talking to him more than you enjoy my society!'

Charity looked miserably at the cold tea in her cup. 'Well, I don't! I don't like him at all! Colin, please talk to him about Alexander soon so that we can go back to England. I don't want to stay here a moment longer than we have to!'

Colin shrugged. 'Suits me,' he agreed. He went back to

eating the piece of seed cake he had in his hand, humping a shoulder in Loukos' direction as he too came over to their table and ordered a fresh pot of tea.

Charity gave him a kick under the table. 'Now!' she whispered. 'Arrange to see him now, or we'll never get away!'

He shrugged again, half turning to face Loukos. 'May I come and see you tomorrow morning, Mr. Papandreous? Charity wants a decision one way or the other, and I must say I agree with her. We can't wait round here for ever.'

Loukos looked from one to the other of them. 'Very well,' he agreed. 'I will see you tomorrow at half past ten in my office. Will that do?

Colin suddenly looked pleased with himself. 'That will do nicely,' he muttered. He winked at Charity. 'What will you do, sweetheart?'

Charity studied her hands, trying not to blush. 'I don't know,' she said. 'I think I may go to Daphni and see the monastery there.'

Colin dismissed her plans with an idle grin, but it was Loukos' reaction which mattered to her. She peeped up at him through her eyelashes and looked hastily away again when she saw the look in his eyes.

'Take a taxi,' he advised her. 'There are buses, but they leave some way away from your hotel. Perhaps, afterwards, you would care to have lunch at my flat and see the baby?'

She nodded quickly, biting her lip as she saw Colin's frown. 'Charity may like to, but you can count me out,' he said abruptly. 'I have other things to do!'

What things? Charity wondered uneasily. But she said nothing. She only hoped that Loukos wouldn't hold his ungraciousness against him, but that was too much to hope for. Even she could see that he didn't like Colin and didn't think him a suitable foster-father for Alexander. She knew as surely as if he had told her then and there that he was not going to allow them to have Alexander. And what was she going to do then? She couldn't possibly marry Colin for *nothing*! In fact she was beginning to think that she couldn't marry Colin whatever Loukos decided. And how to tell him, she really couldn't imagine.

CHAPTER EIGHT

CHARITY went to Daphni on the bus. It was a deliberate act of defiance, which she knew to be childish, but which gave her a certain satisfaction all the same. Because she was not seeing Loukos, she wore the brooch he had given her. It looked particularly well against the soft purple of her sweater and, as she nervously waited for the bus that she hoped would take her to Daphni, she fingered it with delight to give herself courage. The bus, when it came along, was already full. The doors swished open to admit herself and the young priest who had been waiting with her, and they pushed themselves into the back of the bush, exchanging cheerful smiles with the other passengers.

The conductor sat in a little kiosk where he issued the tickets and kept order with splendid impartiality. Seeing the priest, he immediately commanded someone to give up his seat, and the priest sat down, gathering his black robes about him. When he was sitting down, Charity found she could watch him more easily than when he had been standing beside her. He was the first Orthodox priest she had ever seen, and she was fascinated by his stove-pipe hat and the completely Byzantine cast to his face. She was amused to notice the way his long hair was neatly knotted and pinned at the back of his head, and wondered if he used the same kind of hair-grips that she used herself, or whether priests had them specially made for them.

The journey passed quickly. At every stop, the conductor would bend forward and mouth some quite incomprehensible name into the microphone, the doors would swish open, and a few passengers would alight and others get in. Charity began to be afraid that she wouldn't recognize Daphni when it came and she began to move closer to the kiosk, determined to remind him that she wanted to be told where to get out. She need not have worried. When they came to her stop, he reached over the counter in front of him and touched her on the shoulder.

'Daphni!' he announced. She began to push her way towards the door, waiting for it to open and release her. '*Kyria*,' he went on, and pointed across the road and down a narrow side-road opposite. 'Daphni!'

She nodded and thanked him '*Efharisto!*' she called out, wishing that she knew more Greek.

The monastery appeared as a rather forbidding building against the grey sky. There were several trees round the entrance and a taxi waited for some American visitors just inside the gate. Charity smiled at the driver and went on, down a couple of steps, to the ticket office. Hesitantly she inquired in English if she had come to the right place. The woman inside issued her with a ticket and waved a languid hand, ushering her onwards round the monastery.

At first sight, Charity was aware only of disappointment. Was this truly a great example of Byzantine art? It seemed only dark and dreary and extraordinarily difficult to get into. But, once she was inside, she had her first glimpse of the famous mosaic of Christ, so designed that one could stand anywhere in the church and yet the figure of the Pantocrator was never upside down. It was a shame that they were busy carrying out repairs to the fabric of the building, for, without lights, the mosaics were flat and dingy, but she felt she had a very good idea of what they had once been like, gleaming with gold, and covering the walls from top to bottom. In the flickering lights of a hundred candles the figures would come to life, providing a rich, wonderful background to the splendid ceremonial of the Orthodox Church.

Glancing at her watch, Charity was surprised to find how quickly the time had passed. She had scarcely given a thought to Colin's interview with Loukos all morning, but she thought now, staring upwards at the round mosaic of the Pantocrator, of how much she had wanted her own role in life, without being the handmaiden of the rest of her family. Yet here she was, doing her best to gain custody of Alexander, even to the point of agreeing to marry Colin to get him. Being married to Colin was something she had hardly thought about at all. What sort of life would she have? She shivered with cold and the darkness of the interior of the church, and wished that she hadn't thought about it now.

The Americans had left while she had been inside the church and she had the outside completely to herself. A few pillars told that there had once been an even older temple than the Christian one that stood there now. She sat down on one of these pillars and allowed the peace of the place to seep into her, so she was all the more startled when she saw someone coming over the grass towards her and recognized it to be Loukos.

She jumped up, rearranging her face so that he could not notice the mood of self-pity she had drifted into. But of course she didn't bluff him for a moment.

'Thinking of Colin?' he asked her.

'In a way,' she admitted.

'Good. It's time you thought a little further than the wedding ceremony, *pedhi*.'

She blanketed out the distaste she felt for any closer relationship with Colin than that which she had at the moment. 'Are you going to let us have Alexander?' she asked, not quite looking at him.

'No.' Loukos held out his hands to her and she put hers in his as if by instinct. 'Charity, I can't let Colin have the last say in his upbringing. He doesn't want the child for himself—'

'Why else should he want him?' Charity cut him off.

He was silent for a long moment. 'Perhaps because it means so much to you?' he suggested at last.

But Charity shook her head. 'He doesn't understand at

all,' she burst out, only aware of the truth of this herself as she put it into words. 'He doesn't care about Faith, or that she was my sister, or that Alexander needs – needs someone of his own to take care of him!'

Loukos sat down on a second pillar close by the one she had been sitting on and studied her thoughtfully. 'Then have you asked yourself why Colin wants Alexandros?' he asked, almost casually. 'He was very persuasive when he came to see me this morning. Too persuasive,' he added, dismissing the other man with a gesture of his hand.

'I don't think I want to think about it,' Charity said. 'It's only because you don't like him that you won't let me have Alexander!'

'That isn't true. I would allow you to have him, but Colin is something else again. He would have no sympathy for the Greek side of the boy.' He looked Charity steadily in the eyes. 'We will have no argument about it, my dear. I have decided and you will accept it—'

'Why should I?'

He smiled. 'Because it will only make you more miserable each time I refuse you and I suspect you would far rather please me than waste your time setting yourself up against me. True, my Charity?'

'Certainly not!' she gasped.

'How determined you are to deceive yourself, but you do not deceive me!' He reached out a hand and touched her laurel-leaf brooch. 'I am tempted to teach you your true allegiance—'

She looked frightened. 'I haven't got Colin with me now!' she reminded him hastily. 'You promised, Loukos!'

He gave a contemptuous jerk to his head. 'Your chosen protector does little to safeguard you when he is with you,' he commented.

'I can look after myself!' she claimed, her cheeks burning for she could not but think that she hadn't made a very good job of it as far as he was concerned.

Apparently he thought so too. 'If you were my *yinéka*, no other man would kiss you and live. And as for you, you would soon be taught the duty you owe the man to whom you belong. You would not kiss another man again!'

'But I didn't kiss you,' she objected. 'You kissed me!' It was not the best argument she could have chosen, she thought miserably. Why, she had practically agreed with him that it was for the man to command and for the woman to obey, and everything else that went with it!

He gave her an ironic look and it was she who looked away. To be loved by Loukos – why, *anything* would be worth that!

'No doubt I would take your obvious reluctance into consideration,' he said dryly.

He had no right to read her mind as if it were an extension of his own, she thought indignantly. It was equally impossible to allow him the last word. 'I don't know what *yinéka* means,' she complained.

He put a hand under her chin, forcing her to meet the dark brilliance of his eyes. 'No?' he drawled. 'It is something you would very much like to be—'

She stamped her foot at him, her heart pounding with a painful excitement. 'How dare you? You don't know anything about what I want! What I've always wanted! My own life, and my own identity to go with it. That's what I want—'

He laughed, though his amusement was kindly. 'You want what most women want. A man you can love without shame; a man moreover who would enjoy making you his own. Is that sweetness within you really to be thrown away on this cardboard lover of yours? I think not!'

'I – I wanted Alexander,' she attempted to explain.

His smile was very unnerving to her. 'And now that you will not have Alexandros, you will no longer agree to marry this man?'

He was going too fast for her, but she felt impelled to

voice her own doubts about her willingness to marry Colin. 'I don't think so,' she breathed. 'He doesn't seem the same here as he was in England!'

'If you wish to have Alexandros, there is one solution that would enable you to do so. Would you stay in Greece and marry me?'

The hot colour ran up her cheeks. 'But you don't want to marry me! You want someone who wouldn't mind being reduced to being the "woman of your house". A *Greek* woman! I want to live my own life—'

'The choice is yours!' He gave her a look that was so arrogant in its indifference that she was hurt to the quick.

'If – if I married you, you'd let me have Alexander?'

He nodded distantly.

'If I had Alexander, I promise I wouldn't interfere with you at all,' she pressed on, rubbing her brooch between desperate fingers. 'But I don't see why you should want to.'

His expression softened. 'Don't you? Suppose you leave me to worry about that. Do you want to have Alexander with you enough to marry me?'

His use of her nephew's English name made her look up quickly. The warm brilliance of his eyes jerked at her heart. She was not foolish enough to suppose that he would ever love her and she would have to turn a blind eye to any other liaison he might form, such as the one he had enjoyed with Ariadne. She would be hurt and humiliated by her own jealousy, but at least she would be his wife. She blinked, threading her fingers nervously together. He would not allow her a similar freedom, she knew that without being told. If she married him she would have to forget all about having her own path through life. She would have no choice but to follow him wherever he led. Was that what she wanted?

She turned impulsively towards him. 'Loukos, you do like me a little, don't you?'

He put his arm right round her, drawing her close against him. 'Yes, *ylikia*, I like you a little. You will be quite safe with me, you know. I am well able to look after my own.'

She hid her face against his shoulder and found it surprisingly comfortable. He allowed her to stay there for a long time and she was grateful for his understanding, but at last he stirred, making her look up. 'Well, *yinéka*, shall we seal it with a kiss?'

Charity took a deep breath. 'I'll marry you for Alexander,' she said in a voice that sounded quite unlike her own. 'It won't be easy for either of us, but his future has to come first, doesn't it?'

'If you like to put it that way,' he agreed.

She did. She felt it gave a businesslike, impersonal gloss to their future relationship behind which she could hide the melting desire she had to yield to him like wax to a flame. If he had said he loved her— But there was no use crying for the moon!

'I'll have to tell Colin,' she went on, trying not to sound as doubtful about that as she felt. 'Did – did he say anything this morning?'

'What he said this morning was between the two of us. If you are wise, my dear, I should remind him that there was no firm engagement between you and therefore you owe him nothing. He is not above taking advantage of any sign of weakness you present to him.'

Charity smiled. 'Why do you dislike him?' she asked.

He gave her a little shake. 'I shall be glad when you are free of him,' he admitted. 'If there is any trouble, Charity, you are to telephone me at once and I shall make it clear to him that you have a family now—'

Her smile deepened. 'I'm surprised that you are letting me tell him in the first place,' she teased him.

'If you were a Greek woman, I should not,' he retorted. 'But you will be kinder than I should be, and it was you who brought him to Athens and raised his hopes, so I suppose we owe him something.'

She chuckled. 'I may enjoy saying good-bye to him,' she

began, her eyes wide with mischief.

His laughter filled the cloisters. 'I am not afraid! You are signed and sealed with the badge of Apollo!' He touched her brooch and laughed again. 'Poor Charity, stumbling blindly into the path of the gods, to meet your fate. Colin cannot rescue you now, any more than Theseus could rescue Ariadne from Dionysius.'

It was an allusion that she ought to reject out of hand, she thought, and yet— Hadn't Apollo held the Three Graces, the other name for the Fates of the ancient world, in the hollow of his hand, ready to do his bidding?

'I'm only marrying you for Alexander!' she claimed quickly.

He held her by the arms, his fingers biting into her flesh just above the elbows. 'It is your fate to be my *yinéka*, the woman of my house, with or without Alexander. One day I will make you admit as much—'

'*Never!* A woman needs more than—'

He cut off her words with a hard kiss on her mouth that reduced her pride to ashes. What would she do if he ever knew how much she wanted him? 'A woman needs a man to cherish her, as I shall cherish you. If she has that, she must learn to be content with the life her husband marks out for her.'

'But it isn't fair!' Charity gasped, completely outraged by his bland assumption that she would allow herself to be subordinate to him for the rest of her life.

But Loukos only smiled, kissing her again with a thoroughness that made it impossible for her to think of anything but her burning need to respond to his firm touch. Her body arched towards his and she was kissing him as much as he was kissing her. She felt his hand on her hair, sliding down to her shoulder and down her back, holding her closer still. 'Oh, Loukos!' she exclaimed brokenly.

He pushed a lock of red hair away from her face, looking at her intently. 'Would you rather that I were less a man?

That I shared your cold ideas on how a man should treat a woman? But I am a Greek, my dear, and our ideas of marriage are not the same as yours. The man has his role and the woman hers. A Greek woman doesn't question her husband's right to be master in his house and, married to me, nor will you! It is understood?'

She hid her face against him, wanting him to kiss her again. 'Do you have to spell it out?' she complained. She put her hand on the front of his shirt, wondering at the hard warmth of his body. Her fingers trembled and she took her hand back quickly, a little shocked by the strength of her own emotions.

'Yes,' he said. 'I will not have you saying afterwards that you did not know. Greece is not your permissive society in London. When we marry, we stay married no matter what! So, are you prepared to be a Greek wife and put your whole future in my hands?'

Charity bent her head. 'I'll do anything for Alexander!'

He gave her a sharp, angry shake. 'We are not talking about Alexander—'

'Yes!' she burst out. 'Yes, yes, yes! Anything you like!'

He held her away from him, a faint smile touching his lips. 'Was it so hard to say?'

'It wasn't necessary!' she objected.

'Perhaps not.' He pulled her back into his arms. 'But I think it is better said. I have seen the other way with Faith and Nikos. She would never submit to him, yet her defiance gave her little happiness. I will not have my word questioned and doubted, and my wife made miserable and thinking that to escape coming to terms with me she had only to run away and I will give in to her. I will not have my wife falling to her death because she doesn't know that her place is to wait in my house until I come home to her.' He kissed her cheek and then her mouth, murmuring something in Greek, which she couldn't understand but which she found oddly comforting.

'It's getting late,' she said, when she could say anything at all. 'Isn't Electra expecting us for lunch?'

He kissed her one last time, fondling the nape of her neck. 'Getting hungry?' he teased her.

She nodded, though actually she wasn't particularly hungry. She was more afraid of what his kisses might lead to. She was more confused than ever despite his plain speaking. Of course he was marrying her to provide a home for Alexander, just as she was marrying him for the same reason, but why then should he kiss her? Was it just to demonstrate his masculine superiority? She seized on this explanation with something like relief. Once he was sure of her compliance when it came to observing Greek customs, he would leave her alone to get on with the task of looking after Alexander. He couldn't want anything else from her, for he didn't love her, and he had never pretended that he did. So, in a way, she would have a life of her own after all. The only trouble was that she didn't want it.

They went to the car hand in hand. Loukos opened the door for her and shut it on her with a sharp click. She watched him as he walked round the car and her heart turned right over. The fact was, she thought, that she had agreed so tamely to marry him for Alexander's sake because she hadn't the courage to seize hold of her own life even when the opportunity was presented to her. She might have done if she had not fallen in love with Loukos—

She stared at him as he got in beside her as if he were a stranger. He didn't want her love! If she were wise she would back out now and leave Alexander to him. She knew now that she would never marry Colin and, once she was back in England, she would be free. She would have only herself to please for ever and ever! She licked her lips nervously, tearing her eyes away from his face, and knew then that she would never do it. She was committed to Loukos by something stronger than herself. He had only to beckon and she would follow.

She sat up very straight, deliberately analysing the relief that assailed her because she didn't have to worry any more. His support wasn't the kind that would crumble away at the first sign of adversity, as all the other supports in her life had done. She took a deep breath and gave him an insouciant grin, feeling suddenly very pleased with herself.

'You must love Alexander very much,' she observed.

His smile warmed her, giving her pleasure because she liked the way his mouth kicked up in the corners. 'Oh, I do,' he said.

Charity knew she was flattering herself, but it really did seem as though Alexander recognized her and was glad to be nursed by her while he had his midday bottle. Even Electra recognized that there was some kind of tie between aunt and nephew, and was glad of it. Charity supposed that she shouldn't have been surprised by that, but she was a little.

'They are afraid that I shall grow too fond of the baby,' the Greek woman confided with a sad smile. 'They are always afraid for me, but there is no longer any need.'

Charity smoothed the carroty fluff on Alexander's head with a loving hand. 'Why should they be afraid?' she asked.

Electra's black eyes opened wide. 'Have they not told you?' Charity shook her head. 'I thought Loukos was sure to tell you,' the older woman went on. 'After a time it is so much a part of one that one thinks people know just by looking at one. I am growing foolish, no? It must be that I am growing old! Sometimes I look at my sister Xenia, and I think she is old, so I must be growing old too.'

'You seem much younger than your sister!' Charity exclaimed, and then wished that she hadn't. Xenia was Loukos' mother, after all.

'I am a little younger,' Electra admitted. 'We both married very late for this country—'

'I didn't know you had been married?'

'It is seldom spoken of now. I was married before my sister. Two years later I gave birth to a son. He must be thirty-three now. It is all a very long time ago.'

'But he is alive?'

Electra shrugged. 'Who knows? I have not seen him since he was four years old. It was not easy to be in Greece in those times. There were the Communists – and the others. Many people disappeared. Many children were taken into Bulgaria to be brought up as Communists. Dimitri, my son, was taken too, by his father. I have never heard of either of them again.'

'But how dreadful!' Charity exclaimed, appalled.

'It was very bad. I would see a child running in the street and I would think it must be him. It never was. Sometimes the mother would complain that I was trying to take her child away from her and my family became afraid to let me go out by myself. It was hard to see so many beautiful babies and to have my own arms empty. But I was younger then. My son is now a man and I know, even in my heart, that if I saw him in the street he would be a stranger to me. But the family is still afraid for me. They are afraid that I shall grow too fond of Alexandros and come to believe that he is mine. They forget that I am long past such foolishness; that a baby's cry no longer rejoices my heart, but only serves to remind me that my joints are growing stiff and that I sleep too badly now to enjoy having my slumbers disturbed. I want to be a grandmother now, not a mother!' Her staccato English died away into silence. Charity's eyes filled with tears as she looked at her, her unspoken sympathy too deep for words.

'You can always be Alexander's grandmother,' she said gently.

Electra shook her head. 'Xenia is the boy's grandmother. Nikos was her son, just as Loukos is.'

'But Faith's mother—'

'It was a son I had, not a daughter!'

Charity chose to ignore the elder woman's protest. 'You might have had a daughter later on. Besides, children ought to have heaps of relations to love them and spoil them a little. We haven't anyone in our family to do that, so Alexander will need you as well as Xenia!'

Electra gave her a sharp look. 'You are not afraid that I will be bad for the boy, smothering him with too much perverted mother-love?'

'Certainly not!' Charity smiled a little. 'I am expecting you to tell me when I get too sentimental about him. You see, he is so very like Faith!'

Electra sniffed. 'But you will be back in England with that Colin of yours!'

Charity felt herself blushing. 'I – I'm staying in Greece,' she stammered. 'I'm going to marry Loukos—'

'For the sake of your sister's child?'

'Yes,' Charity said, feeling like a traitor.

Electra laughed softly. 'Oho, you think that now, but how will you feel when Loukos makes love to you? He will not be content with a half-hearted woman in his bed! Nor is he a man you can stay indifferent to for very long, no?'

The colour surged up Charity's face. 'It won't be like that!' she said quickly. 'It's – it's a matter of convenience, to give Alexander a home—'

'No man would be content with that for long!' Electra stated with contempt. 'And you? Will Alexander make a woman of you? You will want more than he can give you long before the honeymoon has ended!'

'I – I shall be content—'

Electra uttered a sound of complete disbelief. 'I give you a week of marriage, if that, before you are head over heels in love with him. Loukos will see to that!'

'Perhaps,' Charity hazarded with a humility that hurt her pride but which she couldn't help, 'perhaps Loukos will fall in love with me?'

Electra gave her a kindly smile. 'In a marriage that is less important. Loukos will be kind to you, you can be sure of that! But love? No doubt he loves, or loved, Ariadne. Who can say? But if you are his wife, he will keep such things away from you and his children. You need not know what he is about unless you wish to, and why should you want that? You will have an importance in his life that no other woman can achieve. It is best to be content with that.'

It was probably very good advice, Charity conceded, but she felt chilled by it. If she felt like that now, how would she feel in the years to come? she wondered helplessly, if he didn't come to love her – not as she loved him, she didn't expect that, but she wanted him to be glad that he had married her because he loved her better than anyone else, *better than Ariadne!*

Charity sighed audibly. Alexander had finished his feed and was already dropping off into a deep slumber. It was time for him to go back to his cot, but she put off the moment of getting up, holding him close against her.

'Will Xenia be very angry?' she asked suddenly.

Electra held out her hands for the baby. 'Loukos will be waiting for his lunch!' she declared. 'I can't wait here, gossiping with you. I have other things to do!'

'She will be disappointed, won't she?' Charity insisted.

Electra made an impatient gesture. 'If she is, it will be because your sister never felt at home here. She despised our Greek ways and despised her husband because he was Greek. Xenia did not dislike her, but neither did she welcome her as a daughter-in-law. There was no respect between them.'

Charity bit her lip. 'And she thinks I will be the same?'

Electra's black eyes snapped back at her. 'You are Faith's sister. But Loukos is very different from Nikos, although they were brothers. If you marry a man from another country, you cannot expect him to become English!' She laughed shortly. 'Xenia will welcome you as Loukos' wife if you do the things she expects you to do and respect our customs.'

'The woman of his house,' Charity said dryly.

Electra bent over Alexander's cot, a smile softening her face. 'There are worse things, such as those that I have suffered. Loukos is not Nikos. You will be a Greek wife in the end, whatever you may think now. Poor Faith could never admit that she was a Papandreous, but I think you will not deny it?'

'I suppose not,' Charity said. It was another sign that Apollo had failed her, and that she would never be a person in her own right.

CHAPTER NINE

'YOU'RE going to do *what*? Are you stark, staring mad?'

Charity pursed her lips together in a mutinous line. 'It isn't as though we're in love with one another—' she began.

'What has that got to do with it?' Colin broke in. 'Use your wits, girl! What possible chance of happiness have you got with *him*?'

'I'm not thinking of my own happiness,' Charity declared. 'I'm thinking about Alexander! It isn't *my* fault that you made such a bad impression on Loukos that he won't let you have anything to do with Alexander's upbringing. I have to marry him if I want Faith's baby. And I do!'

Colin shook his head at her. 'So it's a big sacrifice to you, is it?' he asked nastily.

Charity licked her lips, uncertain as to how to answer that. 'N-not exactly,' she compromised. 'It's – only a convenience to make a home for Alexander. I'm sorry, Colin. I know I misled you. I should never have asked you to come—'

'I'm glad you did!'

She stared at him in astonishment. 'Why?' she asked abruptly.

'Perhaps I don't consider you quite lost to me,' he remarked. 'Not yet, at any rate. I have big plans for the two of us, Charity. We're going places, and I know how we're going to get there! It's going to be quite something, carrying off the prize and getting the better of Loukos Papandreous, all in one fell swoop!'

He sounded as though he hated Loukos. Charity felt afraid, but she didn't really believe him. She knew now that Colin was ineffectual and felt that the world owed him something, but the world seldom paid up to that kind of person. And Loukos? Loukos could look after himself – and he would look after her too. She knew that without being told, and the comfortable feeling it gave her made her feel better. She looked up at Colin and smiled.

'What are you going to do?' she asked him.

His eyes narrowed thoughtfully. 'It's better if you don't know. Be quiet a minute, Charity, I'm trying to think about this marriage of yours. It may be just the thing to keep our Greek friend busy, too busy to keep an eye on what I'm doing! Yes, I think it may do very well.' He bowed towards her, smirking a little. 'All right, my dear, you have my consent to play along with him until I'm good and ready. You'll enjoy that, won't you? I've noticed that you like his kisses better than mine, but I don't think you'd really like being married to him. He would own you, body and soul, and you wouldn't like that at all! So I'm afraid you'll have to put up with marriage to me in the long run.' He laughed without humour. 'But you'll have young Alexander to console you. And me? I'll have— Ah, but that would be telling! I'm not going to tell you anything in case you think it your duty to run off to Loukos with the information! You're a loyal little puss, but I'm not sure that your Greek god hasn't blinded you as to your best interests for the moment.' He laughed again. 'It will be something of a relief to get you away from this pagan land, really it will. You're too susceptible to the games they play, as mere mortals always were, I believe, but then I'm not very well up in that sort of thing!'

'I think it's you who's gone mad!' Charity observed. 'Though he *is* like Apollo, isn't he?' she added dreamily.

'Have you fallen in love with him?' Colin demanded.

Charity pulled herself together with an effort. 'I'm quite serious about marrying him. And I don't believe a word of all that rigmarole you've been telling me either. You don't want to marry me, we both know that if we're honest. If you had wanted to, you would have asked me, but you never

131

have, not even in the last few days!'

'I like you well enough,' he protested.

'But I don't like you well enough, Colin. I'm awfully sorry, but I don't. I'm going to marry Loukos and be the woman of his house—'

'What about Ariadne?'

She flushed. 'What about Ariadne?' she countered. 'That's all finished, if you must know—'

'There'll be plenty of others!'

She couldn't hide the hurt his words caused her. As if she didn't know that anyone as attractive as Loukos could have any woman he wanted, married or not! 'I'll have Alexander,' she said doggedly.

His laughter mocked her. 'You'll have me too! But you may as well pretend that you're going to marry him in the meantime. I'm going away for a few days,' he added, 'so feel free to play your part convincingly, my sweet. You won't find me a jealous husband—'

'I wish you'd listen to me!' Charity burst out. 'I mean it, Colin! I'm going to marry Loukos and nothing you do is going to stop me!'

'That's what you think,' he returned with a smug smile. 'When the time comes, you'll fall into my hand like ripe fruit! By the way, I don't think I can quite cover my bill here – do you think Apollo will pay it for me?'

'I shan't ask him!' Charity retorted. 'I'll pay it myself!'

He smiled and nodded. 'Just as you like. I'll be seeing you, Charity my love—'

'No, Colin! Please don't come back!'

'Now that is too much to ask, my dear. I'll be back in a day or so and you'll find you'll be quite pleased to see me after all, so don't look so tragic, my sweet. It'll all come out in the wash. And what a wash!' he added with a gurgle of laughter. ' 'Bye, Charity. Look after yourself!'

Charity watched him go down the steps into the foyer of the hotel. Part of her mind was aware only of relief that he was going. Another part was busy wondering if she hated him, or if it was just a strong spasm of distaste for him brought on by his ridiculous posturing about their future. She thought it might well be hatred. She thought it quite objectively, as though it were not her emotions she was examining at all. If she did hate him, it was because he made her feel that what she felt for Loukos was somehow cheap and temporary, and because he had sneered at Loukos. That had made her truly angry! He could say what he liked about her, but not about Loukos! Why, Loukos was worth ten of him! He wasn't fit to clean Loukos' shoes!

The barman came over and asked her if she would like a drink. She looked up at him vaguely. 'N-no, thank you.'

'The gentleman is coming back?'

She shook her head. The barman picked up Colin's empty glass and went back to the bar. A whole lot of other people had come into the bar in the last few minutes and Charity realized that she could hardly go on sitting there if she didn't have a drink. She rose wearily to her feet and went down to the reception desk, determined to clear up Colin's bill before she did anything else so she wouldn't have to think about him again. He might have said he was coming back, but why should he bother? It had all been hot air, all that he had said, but it had been unpleasant all the same. She wished Loukos had been with her. Indeed, she wished he were here now. Her spirits rose dramatically at the thought of him. He was coming to take her to visit his parents that afternoon and she would tell him then about Colin. Her hands shook a little and she pressed them down on the desk in front of her and smiled deliberately at the hotel clerk.

'Mr. Anderson is leaving today,' she said, a lilt to her voice. 'May I have his bill as soon as it is ready?'

'As you wish, *kyria*.'

She thanked him and turned away to take the lift up to her room. Another hour, or maybe a little less, and she would be with Loukos!

But, in the end, she never mentioned Colin to Loukos at all. The look in his eyes when he came to collect her made her very circumspect in her greeting and not even his obvious amusement would make her do otherwise than offer him her hand and keep her distance from him in the car.

'Have you told your parents yet?' she asked him as they drove through the centre of Athens on their way to Kifisia.

He smiled at her lazily. 'Nervous?'

'Yes, I am, a little. I don't think they liked Faith—'

'That was quite different!'

'But it wasn't really. Faith was my sister and I'm very like her in lots of ways. I can't help thinking they'll be disappointed.'

'You worry far too much,' he told her. 'Nikos was my brother, but our marriage will be quite different from theirs, I can assure you of that! My mother will welcome you as her daughter-in-law if she thinks you will make me happy. She isn't the ogre you imagine her to be. I think she is a little afraid of you too!'

'Of me?' Charity wondered. 'Why should she be?'

'She is afraid you'll challenge her whole way of life and that she won't be able to do anything about it. It wasn't easy for her when all the women began to talk about Faith's independent ways—'

'But Faith would never have caused a real scandal!'

'Not in England perhaps. In Athens, she caused a great deal of talk, first of all by refusing to give up the flat and go with Nikos to Delphi and, later on, by the way she complained about their way of life in Arachova. My mother's friends were all horrified and made all sorts of suggestions as to what Nikos should do to bring her to heel—'

'How horrible!'

He reached out for her hand, threading his fingers through hers. Charity felt her nerves tingling at his touch and had to force herself not to return the pressure of his fingers on hers.

'It wasn't very nice for my mother,' he said dryly.

'It doesn't sound as though it could have been very nice for Faith!' Charity maintained stoutly. 'I'm not surprised she didn't want to live in Arachova!'

His brilliant eyes challenged her. 'If I said we were to live there, would you pack up and follow me there?' he asked.

She was silent, distressed by the question. She would want to follow him anywhere, even to that poverty-stricken house in Arachova. Indeed, she thought it might be preferable to live with him in such a place because there was no room there to be other than companionable. There she would have had to share his bed and his board and she would have *made* him love her! But to say so smacked horribly of disloyalty to Faith, whose circumstances had been different, for she had been sure of Nikos' love and had been pregnant at the time.

'Would you have run away from me?' Loukos insisted, carefully draining all emotion out of his voice.

'No,' she said.

His lips twitched. 'I thought not!'

'How could you know?' she demanded.

He laughed. 'I know a great deal about you, *yinéka* of mine!'

'You couldn't know that,' she said, blushing. 'I don't even really know myself! I may *think* so, but the reality might be quite different!' She bit her lip, aware of his open amusement. Then the title he had given her suddenly struck her, interfering with her breathing in the most uncomfortable way. *His* woman! How she wished she was!

Loukos slipped the car smoothly into the right stream of traffic and rounded the corner into Kifisia.

'The reality is going to be better than you think!' he assured her. 'Which brings me to our wedding, Charity. This half-way house is difficult for both of us, especially for you. Is there any reason why we should delay the ceremony, or are you prepared to marry me as soon as I can arrange the day?'

She thought about it for a moment. It would certainly be easier to meet Loukos' friends in Athens as his wife rather than as Faith's sister, though she would have died rather than admit it to anyone but herself.

'I want to tell Hope,' she said in a smothered voice. 'It would be silly for her to come all the way from America, but I wouldn't like to get married without her knowing.'

'Ah yes, Hope is your other sister. I'll put through a call to her if you give me her number and you can speak to her for as long as you like. Okay?'

'It'll be frightfully expensive!' she pointed out.

He drew up outside his parents' house and switched off the engine. He was smiling when he turned to her. 'I think you deserve that much,' he said, and kissed her on the cheek. 'You don't ask for much for yourself, do you? You were well named Charity – though I can't say the same for that sister of yours!'

'We all hate it!' Charity admitted. 'It's been the bane of our lives! But the others hated it more than I did because they were older. They only had to say their names to be asked, Where's Charity? That was bad enough, but it was even worse when all they could say was that I was at home and wait for them all to laugh at them, as they always did!'

He touched her cheek again with his lips, sliding over her soft skin to her mouth. It began as a casual caress, but her own need for him flared and she forgot everything else except the aching response that rose within her in answer to the deepening demand of his kiss. She was shaken and tearful when he put her away from him. How was she going to survive a platonic marriage when she felt like this about him? What was she to do? He must know the effect he had on her, for he was far more experienced in dealing with her sex than she was with his, and she couldn't help wondering

136

what he thought of her for making it so easy for him to kiss her. The only answer she could dredge up did nothing for her self-respect, and she pulled herself away from him and began to smooth down her hair, not daring to meet his eyes in case what she read there humiliated her still further.

'The quicker I marry you the better!' he said in a funny, tight voice.

She nodded, still not looking at him. 'Electra will be glad. She was telling me—' She broke off, quite unable to continue.

'Oh, Charity!'

'D-don't!' she begged. 'You know we're only getting married because of Alexander!' She wrenched open the door and ran up the garden path to the door, not caring whether he was following her or not, until she felt his hand fall heavily on her shoulder.

'Will you still be telling me that *after* we're married?' he demanded, his anger blazing in his eyes.

She forced herself to be still. 'Of course,' she said. 'It's the truth—' Her voice died away into a painful silence. *It was partly true!* She took a shuddering breath, on the point of going on, to tell him what? But the door opened in front of her and Loukos' father, smiling genially, took her by the hand and led her into the house.

Both Spiro and Xenia were very kind to her that afternoon. In their very limited English they welcomed her to their family and then turned with relief to Greek to discuss the wedding plans with their son. At intervals Xenia would include her with a little nod and a satisfied smile, and then another babble of Greek would break out with all the sound and fury of a full-scale family quarrel. That it was nothing of the sort only dawned on Charity slowly. It seemed that this was the Papandreous way of agreeing with each other and, as she sat silently listening to them, she felt a sudden desire to laugh. It was so very different from the family life she had known, especially after her sisters had gone, and a sad silence had descended between herself and her ailing father. Her eyes met Loukos' and she began to laugh in earnest, to her own consternation and the surprised gratification of everyone else who laughed happily with her, even though they had no idea what they were laughing about.

Loukos put his arm about her and hugged her. 'Is getting married such a joke?' he asked her, his eyes amused.

'Not really,' she admitted. 'It's the way you all shout at each other, and none of you listen to a word anyone else is saying!'

'Very true,' he agreed, 'but we get there in the end. We've even decided on the church for the wedding!'

'Oh,' she said blankly. 'And when?'

'But of course when! Three days from now. My mother insists that you wear her wedding dress, which can be altered to fit you, and my father will stand for you at the altar.' He turned back to his parents with another spate of Greek and she was left to digest this bit of information. It made it seem very close. She stole a shy look at Loukos from under her eyelashes and thought that he was still a stranger to her. What would it be like, living in his flat and seeing him every day? It was bound to be strange. And, no matter how hard she tried, she was bound to irritate him sometimes and she wasn't sure that she could bear his displeasure! *Three days!* It wasn't half long enough for her to get used to her new status in life.

Somehow, the afternoon flew past and it seemed no time at all before she was standing on the doorstep again, embracing her future in-laws, and trying not to think of what lay in store for her. A strange ceremony, in a strange language, and then an even stranger marriage, and all because of Alexander!

She was surprised when Xenia put her arms right round her and kissed her warmly on either cheek. 'I am very pleased,' the Greek woman whispered. 'Electra tells me many things and I am sure you will make Loukos a fine wife. You will make him very happy, yes?'

'I'll try,' Charity heard herself promise.

Xenia chuckled, her dumpy body heaving with laughter. 'Where there is love, trying is not very difficult!' she smiled.

Charity could only stare at her, her eyes wide, but Xenia only laughed the more and patted her hand with her own dimpled one while she said something in Greek to Loukos, who looked at Charity with such intensity that she felt herself blush and looked down at her feet with a shyness she had not felt since she had been about six years old. But Loukos only smiled at her and held her loosely by the wrist all the way to the car.

The next three days passed in a whirl. Xenia's wedding dress fitted her better than anyone could have suspected and needed remarkably little alteration. Charity could only think that Xenia's shape must have changed considerably since the days of her own wedding. It was a dress of ivory-coloured silk, cut on medieval lines, with a square neckline and huge sleeves that fell almost to her feet and which were just like wings when she held her arms aloft. Embroidered with seed pearls and with touches of silver at the neckline and hem, it must have cost a pretty penny when it was new. Xenia agonized over the tarnished silver, but Electra, ever the more practical sister, devised a way of cleaning it to the satisfaction of them both. Charity was too bemused by this time to care deeply about anything. She did what anyone told her to do, trailing in and out of hairdressers, dress-makers, jewellers, and the cake-shops that Xenia loved to visit more than anything else in the world. Of Colin she thought not at all, and of Loukos she tried not to, because even thinking about him set her heart pounding against her ribs and destroyed what little presence of mind she had left.

The night before the wedding she went to stay with Loukos' parents. Loukos came to dinner, which surprised her, for she had thought he would be out celebrating his last night as a single man.

'A stag party?' he had exclaimed, when she had put the idea to him. 'I do not find it very complimentary to the bride that one must go out and get drunk the night before one marries. It is a joke, no?'

She had assured him that no one considered it a joke, but his air of disapproval had remained, to her secret delight, for she found it reassuring that he appeared to welcome marriage to her as something pleasant and didn't think it a prison he was entering for the rest of his life. But then no Greek man would think that, she told herself wryly. It was the wife who was the prisoner in this country, while the man remained free to live exactly as he had before. And here she was, hurrying into jail as fast as she could go, and *she could hardly wait*! There, that was the truth of the matter – she wanted to be Loukos' wife more than anything else in the world!

Loukos had booked her call to Hope in the States. When it came through, he himself spoke to her sister for a long time before he called her to the phone. Charity took the receiver from him with a nervous smile. It had been silly to want to talk to Hope when she had nothing to say to her. She never had!

'H-Hope?' she stammered.

'Darling!' her sister's voice came back, warm, with American overtones, and quite unfamiliar to her. 'I gather you're making the most brilliant marriage of any of the Archers. Well done you!'

Charity felt totally blank. 'Am – am I?'

Hope sounded amused. 'I gather this is a love match too?'

Charity looked about her to make sure that no one was listening. 'I'm in love with Loukos,' she admitted with a rush. 'I'm terribly in love with him!'

'Then that's all right,' Hope said cheerfully. 'He sounds very nice. He says he'll bring you over to the States next time he comes and you can have a long visit with us—'

'Oh!' Charity gasped. 'I shouldn't rely on it. I mean, it would be very expensive, wouldn't it? And then there is Alexander. I have to look after him!'

'Bring him too,' Hope said, unmoved.

'But that would cost even more!' Charity pointed out, much agitated.

Hope laughed. 'My dear, haven't you any idea how much your husband is worth? He's the nearest thing to a million-aire I'll ever know!'

Charity was astounded. 'You mean you've heard of him?' she asked.

'I've travelled on his ships! Oh, Charity, if it isn't just like you not to know a thing like that! Didn't Faith ever tell you—' She caught herself up. 'No, I suppose she didn't, when I come to think of it, because you were so much younger. You know, love, I'm beginning to think Loukos is a lucky man! Does he know that you're not marrying him for his money?'

'I don't know,' Charity said. She turned the subject to Hope's children and then thankfully rang off, feeling more confused than ever. The Papandreous family might have been extremely rich at one time, but there was no sign of any great wealth now – certainly not in the house her sister had lived in in Arachova! Not that it mattered much to her either way. It was Loukos she was going to marry, not his fortune or lack of it.

She thought she wouldn't sleep at all that night, but on the contrary, she fell into a deep slumber the instant her head touched the pillow. When she opened her eyes again, she could hear the muffled sounds of feverish activity going on all round her, and a minute later there was Electra's dour face peering round the door at her with a cross look at her watch and a warning that she would be late at the church unless she hurried herself.

Charity didn't feel like herself at all. She wore her mother-in-law's dress and looked, even to her own eyes, so devastatingly beautiful that her heart missed a beat when she saw her own reflection in the glass. She hoped Loukos would think her beautiful too – more beautiful than Ariadne for instance, and a lot more loving.

She went to the church on Spiro's arm, not knowing what to expect. She had never been in an Orthodox church before and the magnificence of its furnishings made her hesitate for an instant in the doorway. She had an impression of rich, oriental carpets that completely covered the floor, and gold and silver-covered ikons hanging from every available space on the walls, lit by a mass of candles. The priest was dressed from head to foot in cloth of gold, his long hair hanging about his shoulders beneath his golden headdress. She stood beside Loukos, who looked stern and withdrawn, and the butterflies in her own stomach died away and she gave all her attention to the gorgeous ceremony that made her his wife. For what seemed like hours, crowns were held over her and Loukos' head, and a ribbon was threaded about their hands. She had no idea what the blessings meant, but Loukos had arranged for her to repeat her vows in her own language and her voice was strong and clear as she made her promises directly to him.

Afterwards, she stood beside Loukos at the door of his parents' house and welcomed their guests with a fixed smile, wondering who all these people could be. The celebrations went on all day and the Greek flowed back and forth around her with her not understanding a single word of it. Occasionally someone would address a remark to her in English and she would start like a fawn and stand a little closer to Loukos, who would answer for her, giving her a reassuring smile. She found she liked having him beside her, but then she liked everything about him.

It was quite late when the last of the guests had gone and Loukos packed Electra and Alexander into the back seat of the car and then handed her into the seat beside his, still in her wedding finery. She didn't utter a single word the whole way back to his apartment, for a new worry had come to her. She followed Electra into the lift, inordinately relieved that Loukos had still to put away the car.

'I think I'd like to go to bed straight away,' she said to the older woman. Electra only smiled and opened the door of one of the bedrooms, bidding her enter by a nod of her head.

'Sleep well,' was all she said. 'I shall see to Alexander for tonight and until you get used to his ways.'

Charity nodded, feeling depressed. She spent a long time in the bath and an even longer time brushing her hair before she got into bed. It seemed such an anticlimax after all the splendour of the wedding.

Even so, she was quite unprepared for Loukos' entrance when he came into the room. She drew the bedclothes up round her neck and swallowed. 'This my room,' she said faintly.

He raised his eyebrows. 'Yours? Until today it was mine alone, but I'm willing to share it with you. It's a big bed for one as small as you are!'

'But it isn't that sort of marriage! It's only an arrangement – for Alexander!'

'So you keep saying,' he smiled at her, seating himself beside her on the bed. 'I would do much for Alexander, but I can find a nanny for him without having to marry her! You made me certain promises today. Now is the time for you to fulfil those vows. I thought you understood that?'

'Yes,' she said desperately. 'But—'

He moved a little closer and she could feel the warmth of his thigh through the thin bedclothes. 'If I go now it will not be a marriage at all. You will go back to London and Alexander will stay here with me. It will be annulled – finished!

Is that what you want?'

If he had uttered one word of love she would have begged him to stay. But he did not.

'Loukos, I need time. Is that so much to ask?'

He put a possessive hand on her cheek, drawing a line along her jaw and down the curve of her throat to the neckline of her nightdress, bringing the hot colour flooding in the wake of his touch. 'Foolish Charity. Fight me all you want, *ylikia*, it will all be the same in the end.' He kissed her lips with a deliberate ease, holding both her hands in one of his behind her back. She thought her heart would explode within her and that he must surely know it, just as he knew how much she wanted to give way to him. He pulled back a little, smiling into her eyes. 'Well? Do I have a willing wife?'

'You can't make me—' she began. He kissed her again and she was lost. She tore her hands free and wound them round his neck, giving herself up to the delight of his caresses.

'Well?' he said again.

She thought she would drown in the brilliance of his eyes, and it would be the loveliest death imaginable. The radiance of Apollo, with all the glory of the sun to warm her.

'I'd like you to stay,' she said, her voice catching on the words.

'Please,' he prompted her.

She veiled her eyes from him and smiled at him. '*Parakalo*,' she whispered. 'Please, Loukos!'

His answer was in Greek and therefore incomprehensible to her, but there was no doubt at all about the message of his lips on hers and the strength of his arms about her. She kissed him warmly and then she thought, Poor Ariadne, to have lost all this! And then she didn't think at all.

CHAPTER TEN

ALEXANDER was crying. Charity slipped out of bed without
disturbing Loukos. She pulled on her dressing-gown, looking down at his sleeping form, her heart overflowing with
love for him. With his eyes hidden from her, he looked less
like Apollo, but his mouth was as firm and as beautifully
moulded as ever. Alexander began to cry all the harder for
being ignored. Charity smothered a yawn and reluctantly
stopped admiring her husband and went to pick up her
nephew. Electra was right, she thought as she took a clean
nappy out of the drawer. The Greek woman was too old to
be a mother to Alexander. If she could sleep through that
uproar, she could sleep through anything, and the fact was
she ought to be allowed to do just that!

Charity plonked the baby down on her knee, crooning to
him softly as she changed him and put on his day clothes. If
she hurried, she promised herself, she could creep back into
bed before Loukos woke up. The thought made her tremble.
How gentle he had been with her! She had never thought
that the consummation of her marriage could be such a
glorious thing. His patience had been inexhaustible and, if
she had been afraid in that first moment when her body had
accommodated itself to his, she had quickly been carried
away on a passionate tide of love for him, carried far out of
her depth into a new and, to her, completely uncharted sea
that contained only Loukos and the overflowing love she
bore him.

He had soon forced a confession of that love, not once but
many times during the night. It seemed he liked to hear her
say it. But he had never once told her that he returned her
love, not even when he had reached out for her a second, and
then a third time, and had made ardent love to her all over

again.

She had, she remembered, told him other things too, things that she had never told a living soul, things that she had barely known herself. She had told him of her father's long silences and her loneliness when both her sisters had gone away and left her alone to cope with his lengthy illness and finally with his death. She had told him too how she had never succeeded in having an identity of her own. She had spent her whole life being the youngest sister, or her father's daughter, but never anybody in her own right.

Loukos had held her close. 'And now you are to be Alexandros' aunt!' he had teased her.

She had frowned into the darkness. 'I suppose so,' she had said. 'If he hadn't been so like Faith, I'd have turned tail and run back to England as fast as I could go!'

'Never!' he had said, his lips on hers. 'I would have had something to say to that!'

'I love you,' she had said, out loud and quite deliberately. And he had laughed and whispered something in Greek right into her ear, and had kissed her again just as she had hoped he would.

Alexander drank his bottle a great deal too fast and was sick all over her dressing-gown. She cleaned up the mess with mild distaste, telling him just what she thought of him for holding her up when all she wanted to do was get back to Loukos.

'I should have left you to cry yourself back to sleep!' she rebuked him.

'Why didn't you?' Loukos said from the doorway. His hair was still awry from sleeping, his feet were bare, and he was still in the process of putting on his dressing-gown.

She flushed at the sight of him, a little shocked that he should wander about the apartment practically naked. 'Electra will see you!' she warned him.

He laughed out loud, coming over to her and slipping his hand beneath the curtain of her hair to caress the nape of her neck. 'Are you going to be as jealous as you are passionate?' he chuckled.

She held up her face readily for his kiss. 'I hope not,' she said soberly. 'I've always thought jealousy was the sign of a small mind!'

'Mmm.' He kissed her thoughtfully. 'Not in a woman. All women are jealous where they love.'

'And men aren't?' she countered somewhat tartly.

He laughed again. 'It is in a man's own hands to see that his wife gives him nothing to be jealous about!'

She gave him a melting look. 'Then you don't think you have anything to worry about?'

The twinkle in his eye made her cheeks hot. 'Not very much,' he drawled and, taking Alexander out of her arms, pulled her close against him. 'Do you?'

She smiled, shaking her head. 'No,' she admitted. 'It's quite unseemly how much I love you!'

He considered her choice of words with an arrogant tilt of his head while he placed the baby back in his cot. 'Unseemly,' he repeated, liking it. 'Good! That is how it ought to be!' He came back to her and kissed her soundly, breaking off only when they heard Electra's footsteps coming towards them in the corridor outside.

Electra was apologetic that she hadn't heard Alexander's cries. 'It was such a busy day yesterday,' she explained, 'and I couldn't sleep, so I took one of Xenia's pills. I must have coffee to wake me up! Have you both had breakfast, or shall I make you some?'

Loukos kissed his aunt's cheek. 'I was hoping someone would feed me soon,' he teased. 'What are you going to have, Charity? I have never asked you before, do you want to have eggs and bacon, toast and marmalade? Or will you eat rolls and coffee with me?'

Charity didn't hesitate. 'Rolls and coffee, please.' She wished she had the courage to say that she would get Loukos' breakfast, but she was afraid of hurting Electra's feelings. It didn't seem much like a honeymoon at all with both her and the baby in the apartment with them, but as Loukos appeared to take it as a matter of course that his aunt should be there, Charity didn't feel in any position to object. She looked across the room at her husband and was struck anew by his gold-tanned skin and the beauty of his perfectly shaped, brilliant eyes. He really was Apollo come to life! She was seized by an urge to visit the Parthenon and see for herself the statue of Apollo that had been represented on the cover of the book she had been reading when she had first seen him. She would like to see if it was as like him as she imagined it to be.

'Loukos, may we visit the Acropolis today?' she hazarded, just as Electra began to pour out their coffee.

Loukos looked at his watch and shook his head. 'This afternoon, if you like,' he said, 'but I have something I must do this morning.' His mouth kicked up at the corners into a smile. 'I should have done it yesterday, but I was otherwise engaged!'

Charity didn't say another word. It wasn't as though he could help it, but she did wish that they could have had a few days to themselves: a few days in which she could have grown used to loving him and, maybe, even have persuaded him that he not only wanted to possess her, but that he loved her a little too.

Whereas, instead of loving her, he seemed to have forgotten all about her. He sugared his coffee and stirred it without even looking at it, his mind elsewhere. Electra handed him the morning's paper and he made a play of reading it so that Charity could no longer see his face. She tried to content herself by working out in her mind the sounds that the various strange letters of the Greek alphabet represented. She began to be afraid that she would never be able to read it, let alone speak it! It looked hideously complicated and not at all like English.

Loukos finished his coffee, folded the paper, and rose to

his feet without a backward glance. Charity blinked away the tears that came into her eyes and pretended an interest she was far from feeling in the sugar bowl in front of her.

'What did you expect?' Electra asked her with a bracing frankness. 'His work has always come first with him, and it won't be different now.'

Charity thought of what Hope had said on the telephone. 'I only wanted a few days,' she said. 'Hope says that he has a great deal of money, so surely he could take a few days off!'

Electra shook her head in wonder. 'Did you need your sister to tell you that Loukos is a rich man? He is not Aristotle Onassis, but the Papandreous Shipping Line is well known all over the world. Spiro retired years ago and Nikos turned his back on the firm. It all came to Loukos then and with it a great deal of responsibility. A great deal depends on him. He can't come and go to please his wife. It is she who must fit in with his work.'

'I know! But not the day after our wedding!'

'You are as spoilt as your sister!' Electra snapped impatiently. 'What do you want from him? That he should do nothing but pander to you?'

Charity sighed. All she wanted was that he should love her – not as much as she loved him, but enough to want to be with her this particular day, and to make love to her again as he had last night.

Electra gave her a not unkind half-smile. 'Have some more coffee! There is washing to be done for Alexandros, and Loukos has a button off one of his shirts. Am I to do it, or will you?'

This was settling down to married life with a vengeance! Charity laughed suddenly. It served her right, she thought, for being sorry for herself! 'I'll do it,' she said. 'Every last bit of it! I can always go to the Acropolis some other time. If I'm going to live here, I'll probably get sick of the sight of it!'

'Oh no, never that,' Electra assured her. 'Loukos will take you this afternoon and I will look after Alexandros for you, but this morning I must visit my sister and see how she is after yesterday. She is not very well these days and it is no good for her to get too tired.'

Charity looked anxious. 'Will you give her my love? She was so kind to me yesterday, and I couldn't bear her to suffer for that!'

'I will tell her,' Electra promised.

Charity gathered up the washing and put it in the sink. She heard Electra going out the front door and Loukos whistling to himself in the living-room. It wouldn't do the nappies any harm to soak for a bit, she thought, and she hurried down the corridor to the bedroom to get dressed before she began the washing in earnest. She had hardly begun to put on her clothes, however, when the front door bell rang imperiously throughout the flat, making her jump. She reached out for the dressing-gown she had just taken off, when she heard Loukos' voice in the hall raised in greeting. Whoever the visitor was sounded more than welcome!

She finished dressing in a hurry, thinking that she would offer whoever had come some coffee. She knew really that it was an excuse for seeing Loukos for a few minutes, but she wanted to show herself as being hospitable as well, so perhaps he wouldn't mind the interruption.

The living-room door was shut. She hesitated outside for a moment and then opened it quietly, pushing it open a few inches, her eyes seeking Loukos' to find out from him if she would be welcome. It was then that she saw him, not seated on one of the chairs as she had expected, but standing by the window with Ariadne in his arms. And he was kissing her. She had her arms round his neck and was pressing herself against him, her eyes tight shut.

Charity shut the door again, feeling physically sick. She tried to tell herself that she had known it all the time, but she had never seen them together, alone, before. It was the end of all her dreams! How could she make him love her when he felt like that about Ariadne? He must love her very much if he could kiss her like that this morning when last night—! But she wouldn't think about last night. She would not!

She went back to the kitchen and did the washing like an automaton, the tears pouring down her cheeks and mingling with the soap-suds in the sink. When she had finished, her head had begun to ache and Alexander had started to cry again. She glared at Loukos' buttonless shirt and threw it quite deliberately on the floor. She would not sew on his buttons! Or do anything else for him! She wouldn't even stay in the same apartment with him, not while he had that woman with him! She would take Alexander and she would go somewhere for the day where he would never find her, and he was welcome to Ariadne – only she couldn't help hoping that some miracle would occur and he wouldn't want her after all and that it would somehow all come right, and she, and not the Greek girl, would prove to be the love of his life that very afternoon!

She went into Alexander's room and he stopped crying, gurgling contentedly up at her.

'It was you who began all this!' she told him tearfully. 'Are you coming with me, or are you going to stay?'

The baby waved his fat little hands in the air and looked as though he might be sick again.

'You've no choice,' Charity muttered, wiping his face for him. 'I can't leave you here on your own all morning!'

She was still crying when she picked up the baby and transferred him to his carry-cot. She struggled into her coat, her eyes misted over with her tears, and went out of the flat, slamming the door behind her. She hadn't even got a key, she thought disconsolately, so she couldn't go back even if she wanted to, for nothing would make her ring the bell and interrupt Loukos' idyll with Ariadne! She pushed the carry-cot ahead of her into the lift, making Alexander cry with fright as his mattress landed on the floor.

'Oh, shut up!' she begged him. 'Please, Alexander! I want to spend the day with him just as much as you do, but we can't!' The carry-cot was heavier than she had expected and she was so busy crying that she couldn't see what she was doing. She had no idea where she was going and she didn't care! She grasped the handles more securely and stepped out of the lift, almost running as she hurried out into the street and the fitful sunlight, and straight into Colin's outstretched arms.

'How's that for timing?' He took the cot from her and smiled at her. 'I was just wondering if I should come up and take a chance on your being alone. They told me at the hotel you'd moved out from there.'

Charity nodded, unable to say anything at all. She accepted his kiss with a frozen dignity and wished he would go away. Couldn't he see that she was perfectly miserable and that the last person she wanted to see was Colin Anderson? But he obviously saw nothing of the kind!

'I've got a car round the corner,' he went on, sounding very sure of himself. 'I thought we might fill in the time by having a picnic. It isn't exactly hot, but at least the sun is shining. Will that suit you?'

Charity shrugged her shoulders. She might as well, she thought. She had nothing better to do. 'Where will we go?' she asked.

'How about Hymettus, where the honey comes from? You look as though you could do with something to sweeten your life right now, and I'm just the man to supply it!'

Charity was immediately intrigued. 'Oh yes, do let's!' she exclaimed. 'The Greeks believed that the very first bees in the world came from there. Do you think it can be true?'

Colin shivered elaborately. 'We'll be lucky if we see a bee today! They'll be hibernating, or whatever bees do in the winter.'

'They filled Plato's mouth with Hymettus honey at birth,' she said. 'I wonder if Alexander would like some.'

'I think one Plato is all the world can stand,' Colin answered. 'What have you been crying about?' he added on much the same note.

'I was just being silly!'

He turned her round to face him, swinging the carry-cot against her legs and making her cry out. 'Did you play Loukos along as I told you to? I see you're looking after the child, which is mightily convenient for us, but what made you move into Loukos' apartment? I thought you'd be more careful of your reputation than that!'

'But I told you I was going to marry him—'

'You're going to marry me!' he bit out. 'It's all part of the plan!'

'But I can't!' Her eyes widened as she saw the blind rage on his face and she was suddenly afraid. 'Colin – it can't matter to you! You never really wanted to marry me!'

He took her by the arm and forcibly marched her round the corner to where he had left his hired car. 'Get in!' he commanded. 'We can't talk about it here!'

Charity struggled feebly against him. 'But, Colin, I have to tell you – I'm married to him! I married him yesterday!'

He let go her arm and she rubbed the place where he had held her, not looking at him. 'Get in!' he repeated.

'But there's no point—'

He raised his hand and slapped her hard. Her head snapped back and hit the roof of the car with a resounding crack. 'Get in! You may have married him, but I'm not going to let you spoil all my plans! You can get an annulment, my dear Charity, and like it!'

'I won't!' she said.

'Oh, for heaven's sake, get in the car! Or do you want a bit more of the strong-arm stuff?'

She put a hand up and felt the side of her face where she

had hit the car. It was already swollen and throbbing painfully. 'But why, Colin? Why?'

He pulled open the front door and gestured her to sit down quickly. He slammed the door after her, catching her skirt in the door and tearing it. With an equal lack of care he tossed Alexander's carry-cot on the back seat and climbed into the driver's seat. He had never driven well, but Charity had never known him drive as badly as he did when he set the car in motion and drove out into the traffic, ignoring the maelstrom of vehicles that whirled about him, blowing their horns and shaking their fists at him.

'Please, Colin, I want to go home!'

'You will, my dear. I've booked all three of us on the evening flight to Paris, and on to London in the morning.'

'I mean home to Loukos!' Charity gulped.

'His home will never be yours!'

But it already was! Charity tried to ease her aching head by holding it with her hand, but it went on throbbing just the same. 'I won't go back to England with you! I won't go anywhere with you! I can't think what's got into you. I told you I was marrying Loukos—'

'I thought it better to play along with the idea until I'd made all my plans. Besides, I never thought he'd actually marry you. A bit of fun maybe, but one Archer had already antagonized his family without his marrying another one of them. He was pretty clear when he spoke to me that he wasn't going to let you get your hands on Alexander!'

'That was when he thought I might marry you!'

Colin smiled without humour. 'I know that! He likes me as little as I do him! I could have laughed all the time he was talking to me. He suspected that I knew about the money, of course, but he couldn't prove it no matter how he tried to make me give myself away! I've been busy checking up on him ever since.'

'Oh no!' Charity protested.

'What's the matter, my sweet? Don't you want a share of

a million pounds?'

'*No!*'

Of course you do! And it's just sitting there, waiting for us to pick it up. I could have kissed you when you walked out of that door this morning and handed me the carry-cot and a million quid with it!'

'I don't believe it!'

His eyes slid over her. 'Why not?'

'You forget, I saw where Nikos and Faith had been living in Arachova. When Nikos gave up work, he gave up all claim to the family fortune. He must have done! No one would have chosen to live in a house like that if they didn't have to!'

'Rubbish, my dear. Nikos didn't leave a will, but his fortune went straight to Alexander and none of the family is contesting it. Forty million drachmas, to be exact! We may not like each other very much, but I think that will hold us together, don't you?'

'*Alexander's money?*'

'Our money. Once we've got him to England there isn't a court in the land that won't give you custody of your sister's son. He needs a woman's care at his age!'

Charity laughed shortly. 'I don't believe for a minute that Alexander has any money, but even if he has, do you imagine that I would touch a penny of it?'

'You will, sweetie, you will, just as you'll get on that plane this evening. You'll do it, because you'll be too afraid not to!'

Judging by the way her head ached, she thought he meant what he said. She felt awful! And somehow she had to think of some way of getting away from Colin. It wouldn't be easy with Alexander, and with Colin himself watching her every step of the way. The only thing she could do was to try and lull him into a false sense of security about her. It went against the grain to talk to him at all, but she gritted her teeth and forced herself to make a start.

'As long as I have Alexander—'

Colin gave a triumphant shout. 'Not as deeply in love with your Greek as you thought, are you? Isn't it marvellous what a million pounds will do!'

'Isn't it?' she said dryly.

Colin took his hand off the steering-wheel and patted her knee. 'It won't be half as bad as you think!' he comforted her. 'Let's talk about it later, Charity. We have the whole afternoon in front of us. Shall we enjoy our picnic first?'

She nodded listlessly. She opened her handbag and took out a comb, looking at her face in the small glass of her powder compact. Her cheek was badly swollen and already discoloured to a dirty shade of black-brown. She thought that by the morrow she would have a black eye as well – and what would Loukos say to that? She sniffed, trying to hold back the tears that the mere thought of Loukos threatened to release. Supposing he thought she had gone willingly with Colin? What would she do then? He would never forgive her, never! And she didn't blame him! She would have been much better employed sewing on the button on his shirt!

The road to Hymettus went through the working class suburb of Kaisariani, which had earned the nickname of the 'Stalingrad of Greece' as one of the chief Communist strongholds in the rebellion of 1944. Charity stared dully out of the window, wondering about the people who lived there now. If Electra's son, Dimitri, ever came back to Greece, was that where he would choose to live? Or would he now feel a foreigner in his homeland, speaking another language, and living all his life away from home? Perhaps he would feel as bewildered as she felt by Greece? Perhaps he would come to love it just as she did? She gave herself a little mental shake, because if she began to think about Greece, she would start thinking about Loukos, and how much she loved him. If only she had not seen him and Ariadne together, she would still be comfortably in his apartment, waiting for him to come to her. But now he would think her another Faith, rushing out of the house because her feelings had been hurt in just the way her sister had. It would serve her right if he *never* forgave her!

The suburb gave way to a small green valley folded into the side of the smooth-topped mountain. There were a number of cypress, plane, and olive trees adding their different greens to the pretty scene. Looking back to Athens, one could see literally hundreds of cream-coloured buildings, all of them similar in design and all of them built in the last few years in an attempt to come to terms with the exploding population of the city.

Colin pointed up the valley to a large plane tree. 'I thought we'd have our picnic up there,' he said. 'I came up here the other day and thought it would appeal to you. There's a spring there.'

'I know,' Charity said.

Colin threw her a quick look of concern. 'Have you been here before?' he demanded.

'No. I read about it. That's the funny thing about Greece, wherever one goes one of them was there before one, way back, probably some time B.C., and it's hardly changed at all. It gives one a funny feeling!'

'I'd give up reading, if I were you!' Colin advised.

'But I want to know!' Charity retorted before she had thought what she was saying. 'It's all part of Loukos, you see—'

Colin turned on her angrily. 'Can't you talk about anything else? If you mention him again, I'll – I'll—'

'Yes? What will you do? Hit me again?'

'I didn't mean to hurt you,' he said sourly. 'You've always been stubbornly unreasonable about the things that matter!'

'Like money?'

He shrugged his shoulders, looking like a hurt small boy. 'I thought you'd like it up here. You haven't even looked at that little monastery over there, and I thought you liked that sort of thing.'

'I do,' Charity said.

'Well then, why do you have to keep talking about Loukos Papandreous?'

Charity got out of the car and walked up the valley towards the spring – a fertility spring, she remembered. Would it work for her? She trembled at the thought of bearing Loukos' child and put it hastily out of her mind. It was water, and it would do to bathe her face in. She heard Colin's footsteps behind her, but she made no effort to turn round. It was bliss to feel the cool fluid on her throbbing head, and he would just have to wait until she was finished.

'Are you in love with him?' he asked her.

'I thought you didn't want to talk about him,' she said. 'You know, Colin, this place is exactly as Ovid described it, except for the monastery, of course. But he called them the purple, flowery hills of Hymettus, and this a sacred spring, and ground soft with green turf. Even Pindar called Athens the violet-crowned citadel of the gods. Hymettus must have meant a great deal to them, don't you think?'

'And Loukos Papandreous is an Athenian!'

'Yes.'

'And you're in love with him?'

She straightened up. 'Hadn't you better fetch Alexander?' she suggested pleasantly. 'I hope you've brought some milk for him. He's a little young for anything else.'

'I didn't bring anything, if you must know!' Colin almost shouted at her, his voice tinged with desperation. 'I thought we could find a restaurant somewhere, after I'd brought you here. I thought you'd think this a sufficiently romantic place to listen to my plans for our future together, but you're in love with that Greek fellow, aren't you?'

'Yes, I am,' Charity said.

Colin clenched his fists. 'It doesn't make any difference! I'm not going to give up a million pounds now that I've

158

come this close to it! You may have married him, but you'll have to get an annulment. It shouldn't be hard, seeing that it's only a convenience so that you can look after Alexander at no cost to him!'

'Is that what you think?' she asked in light, amused tones. 'How little you know about either of us!'

Colin flushed angrily. 'What do you mean?'

'What do you suppose I mean?' She stared at him across the water, raising her eyebrows in mute inquiry. 'Can you imagine Loukos marrying for any other reason?'

'And you let him? How could you, Charity? I told you I'd be back in a few days and that it would be all right then. Whatever made you marry him?'

Charity gave him an exasperated glance. 'Because he asked me to! Besides,' she added, 'I wanted to – very much! I'm *proud* to be his wife!'

Colin's lip curled. 'I'm surprised you can stomach being called Mrs. Papandreous!'

Charity's heart jerked within her. Was she really that? 'I like it,' she said with a certainty that surprised her as much as it surprised Colin. 'And I have no intention of getting an annulment, even if I could, but I'm glad to say that there's no chance of that. So what are you going to do now, Colin Anderson? Take me home to my husband?'

CHAPTER ELEVEN

'Oh no, Miss Archer, I'm not letting you and the money get away from me as easily as that—'

'I'm not Miss Archer any longer,' Charity said proudly. She tossed back her head in a very creditable imitation of the gesture she had once seen Loukos use. 'I'm Mrs. Papandreous!'

'Not for long, sweetie. Not for long!'

Charity strove to retain her air of calm certainty, but inwardly she was not at all sure. 'You can't undo my marriage!' she exclaimed.

'I shan't have to,' Colin assured her. 'Loukos will do that for me. You know that as well as I do, don't you? He has the pride of the devil! What will he have to say at your running round the countryside with me? Have you thought of that? Oh no, my pet, once I have you on that plane, I shan't have to worry any more about your marriage! He'll cast you off quicker than he changes his shirt! And after Faith's disastrous challenge against the Papandreous authority, who will believe you when you say you didn't want to go with me?'

No one, Charity acknowledged. Just as they had not understood what had driven Faith to rush away from the Arachova house when it was her husband's home, so they would condemn her for going away with Colin.

'You can't make me go!' She hesitated. 'I haven't got my passport with me – and Alexander hasn't got a passport at all.'

'You must think me a fool,' Colin smiled. 'I've been planning this for days, sweet Charity. Nothing is going to go wrong now.'

'If you've put us on your passport, it's illegal!' she

declared.

To her dismay, he only laughed. 'Tell that to passport control!' he mocked her. 'If you can.'

'Wh-what do you mean?'

'You'll see!' He splashed his fingers through the water of the spring, a curious smile on his face. 'Do you mean to go on arguing for the rest of the day, or shall we make the best of things and go and take a look at the view before we go and get ourselves something to eat?'

There didn't seem to be anything else she could do. 'We can't leave Alexander on his own in the car,' she managed.

'Why not? He can sleep there as well as anywhere else and he's too young to do anything else!'

Charity shrugged, more miserable than she ever remembered being. Nothing mattered to her any more. Colin took her by the hand and was immediately irritated by the way she winced away from him.

'It's a good thing I'm not a jealous man, but you'll have to do better than that! Relax, Charity! There's nothing you can do to change things now. I may not be the husband you want, but I'm all you're going to get—' He broke off as they came level to the deserted monastery of Kaisariani. 'Do you want to take a look at that church?' he asked her.

She shook her head. 'I don't want to go anywhere with you!'

'Too bad! Perhaps a little exercise will sweeten you. We'll climb up to the top and see what the view is like.' He pushed her ahead of him up the steep slope where he could keep a watch on her every movement. Charity began to walk, bitterly aware of him coming along behind her. There was nowhere where she could hide from him, and her head ached, making it impossible for her to think clearly.

The stunted shrubs of the mountainside whipped against her legs, tearing her stockings to shreds. She began to name them to herself – anything rather than allow herself to think of Loukos' condemnation of her. There was juniper and terebinth, and another shrub she didn't recognize though the name cistus kept coming into her mind. It was hard to tell what all the herbs were in winter. Rosemary, thyme, lavender and aromatic sage, she thought she recognized them all. Ovid had mentioned bays and dark myrtles too, but she didn't recognize either of them, nor the thin lucerne and the cultivated pine. Nor was there any sign of the grape hyacinths and the purple spring crocus, on which the famous bees were supposed to feed. But then it was winter now and the monks who had kept the bees had gone away. The city had grown right up to the mountainside and it was hard to remember that once the Athenians had come up here to escape the ravages of the plague during the Turkish occupation.

They went past another little Byzantine church, with Charity still walking a few paces ahead. She wanted to pause, to catch her breath, but the knowledge that Colin was close behind her made her press on to the summit where the slope flattened out into a rather bleak plateau from where she could look down on the whole of Attica and the islands of the Saronic Gulf. That was Loukos' country – and her own by right of marriage! Let Colin do his worst, she would never leave it! Her heart pounded in time to her panting breath, and she knew that it was partly excitement. If she could inveigle Colin into standing very close beside her, she could push him down that slope and be off down the hill, back to the monastery, before he could recover. She turned to him and forced a smile.

'Isn't it marvellous?' she enthused. 'Oh, Colin, thank you for bringing me here! I'm sorry if I was difficult, but I thought you'd gone away and left me, and that hurt – a little. But if you can truly give me Alexander—' She allowed her voice to die away, despising herself for the little scene she was playing.

'I thought the money would talk to you in the end!' He came and stood beside her. 'Loukos looks less attractive to you all the time, doesn't he?'

She couldn't bring herself to agree, so she looked away from him, right across that magnificent view instead. 'I've always been fond of you,' she began.

He came close. She could feel his breath against her bruised cheek and she hated him. He leaned towards her and she braced herself for the moment when she could tip him off balance. He smiled, and the moment came. She pushed him with all her strength, nearly going with him as he gave her an astonished, hurt look, slipping to his knees. She reached down and pushed him again. It was a defiant, more than an effective gesture, for she had never been particularly strong, but her luck held and he slipped further down the slope, giving her a few extra yards' start in her run for the shelter of the monastery.

The scrubby bushes held her back, laying traps for her feet, and tearing at her clothes, delaying her progress. She kept repeating Loukos' name as if it were some sort of charm to keep her safe as she hurtled on down the steep path. She fell heavily and rolled headlong into a thorny bush, but pulled herself back on to her feet, ignoring her grazed elbows and knees as she pressed on for the bottom.

It was only when the monastery came in sight, the church built in alternating courses of stone and brick which made it instantly recognizeable, that she realized that there was no sign of Colin behind her. She couldn't bring herself to stop and look back up the hill she had just come down, but she changed her mind about hiding in the church as she had first intended and hurried on past the spring to the car and Alexander.

The keys of the car were in Colin's pocket and although she had once seen in a film how to start a car without an ignition key, she was sure that she would never manage such a feat in real life. She pulled open the rear door of the car and reached into the carry-cot for Alexander, overwhelmed with relief to find him safe and still sleeping. She would leave the carry-cot, she thought, and hope that Colin would not look inside it and find the baby gone. If he thought Alexander was there, he would think that she must be somewhere close by too and would waste time looking for her, whereas she hoped to gain the streets of the suburb of Kaisariani and lose herself amongst the other people of the district.

But she had forgotten that these same streets, which had looked so busy when they had driven through them, would now be deserted for the long lunch hour. No matter where she looked, there was no one to be seen anywhere. She soothed Alexander, who had now woken up and was crying for his food, and wondered what to do next. The depressing certainty that Colin would have reached the car by now and would overtake her at any moment began to obsess her. She could not go on much longer. Her body felt battered and bruised and Alexander grew heavier by the moment. She could cry when she thought how close she had come to escaping Colin. If she were to fail now—

She looked up and saw a taxi coming towards her. It was so unexpected that it had almost gone past her before she pulled herself together sufficiently to hail it. It came to a screeching stop beside her, the driver giving her a jaunty look of appreciation that made her more conscious than ever of the state of her clothes and the bruise on her face. With leaden limbs, Charity sank into the back seat and eased Alexander more comfortably on her knee.

'Vasileos Konstantinou,' she murmured to the driver, hoping against hope that he would understand her atrocious accent.

He did not. He smiled encouragingly, winking a knowing eye. '*Pou?*'

'Konstantinou,' she repeated. 'The American Embassy, do you know that?' He looked more confused than ever and reached for a map in the pocket in front of him, passing it to her for her to look at. With some difficulty she found the right place and his brow cleared as if by magic. It was then that she realized that somewhere on Hymettus she had lost her bag, and she hadn't as much as a penny piece on her. She watched the tariff ticking upwards with a fascinated guilt, wondering how she was going to explain it all to the driver.

To add to her trouble, Alexander began to yell. He was hungry and he needed changing, and he was prepared to tell the world all about it in loud, gusty sobs that had no right to be coming from anyone as young as he was. Charity rocked him gently against her, singing to him softly under her breath, but now that he was fully awake, he was not to be soothed so easily. He pounded his legs back and forth against her, curling his toes in his indignation and beating his hands against the empty air.

'Vasileos Konstantinou,' the taxi-driver announced.

Charity gestured him on, pointing out the block where Loukos' apartment was situated. 'Kyrios Papandreous,' she said hopefully. She pointed to her wedding-ring and then to herself. 'Kyria Papandreous!'

The driver smiled, nodding his head vigorously. *'Hero poli pou sas hnorizo!'*

'You don't understand,' Charity said, meaning that she didn't. Her memory for anything she had seen written down was usually good, so she tried desperately to recall something from her Greek phrase book, anything that would help her out now. *'Parakalo perimenete os otou epistrepso,'* she experimented. The driver's suspicious look convinced her that she had not said what she had intended. *'This is ghastly!'*

'Tha ithela no sas sinodhefso,' he said with decision.

Charity wondered what on earth he had said. She gave him a blank look and started to get out of the car. Her legs hurt and she stumbled and almost fell as she stood up. The taxi-driver got out of the car as well.

'Pou piyenete?' he asked her.

That she thought she did understand. Where was she going? She pointed vaguely upwards. 'Kyrios Papandreous,' she said very slowly.

The man nodded. He reached out and took Alexander from her, getting back into the taxi with the baby in his arms.

'But you can't do that!' she exclaimed.

He held the baby away from him, jerking his head towards the American Embassy. 'Americaniki Presvia,' he said.

Charity despaired, 'But that isn't what I want! I must have the baby! It's going to be awful enough—' A great sob shook her and she turned away. If only her head would stop aching and allow her to *think*! 'Oh, all right,' she stormed, 'keep him as a hostage, but don't you dare go away until I get back!' After which remarkably silly speech seeing that he hadn't understood one word of it, she burst into tears and ran up the steps and through the great door that guarded the entrance to the block of flats.

The lift whirred upwards and she stumbled out, going over to Loukos' front door with a little rush and pressing the bell with an urgency that hurt her head. She felt sick and had the horrid feeling that she was going to faint, and wasn't anyone *ever going to open the door*? Supposing they had all gone out? What was she to do?

The door opened a crack and was then flung wide and she found herself in the warm security of Loukos' arms.

'I'm so sorry, Loukos!' she wept. 'I was going to be back by lunchtime, truly I was. I didn't mean—' She gulped, wishing that she could stop crying.

'Slowly, slowly, *agapi mou*,' he whispered. 'Where have you been?'

She took a deep, shuddering breath. 'With Colin,' she confessed. 'Only, I didn't mean to go with him!' She stole a look at him, but she couldn't tell what he was thinking. 'Alexander is in a taxi downstairs,' she said blankly. 'I hadn't any money to pay the driver, you see, and I couldn't understand what he was saying.'

'Naturally not,' her husband said. 'I shall go downstairs and pay him and Electra will look after Alexander. You will sit down and be fussed over by my mother until I get back. No, no—' as she tried to speak again, '—I will hear all about it when I get back, and when you are a little calmer, yes?'

She sniffed and nodded. 'Oh, Loukos, you don't know how sorry I am! I should never have gone out—'

He gave her a little push towards the living-room. 'My mother is in there. And, Charity, no more tears!'

Xenia jumped to her feet with a shocked sound when she saw her daughter-in-law. 'You must sit down at once!' she bade her, beating the cushions into greater comfort with ineffectual, fluttery movements of her pudgy hands. 'That such dreadful things should happen! I will fetch Electra and she will make tea for us both, and we will not cry any more, because it is not the thing when the men are round. They are not understanding and think it tiresome, no?'

Charity blew her nose and tried to laugh. 'I expect you're right,' she said. 'Oh, my head!'

Xenia put her head on one side and peered at Charity's bruise. 'Has Loukos seen this?' she demanded. She clicked her tongue, her eyes flashing with indignation, and called out to Electra in a flood of Greek. Electra answered more calmly from the hallway, but she too exclaimed over the darkening patch on Charity's cheek.

'Loukos will not be pleased!' she said tautly.

Charity bit her lip. 'It was all my fault!' she repeated.

'What will not please me?' Loukos asked from the door-way. He put Alexander into Electra's waiting arms and strode across the room towards Charity. He put a hand beneath her chin and turned her face towards him. A muscle flickered by his mouth as he touched the bruise with fingers so gentle that she could hardly feel them.

'Who dared do this to you? Who dared to hurt you so? Was it Colin?'

She winced. 'It – it doesn't matter!' she assured him.

His hand beneath her chin tightened. 'Not matter? When he has hurt *you*! Do you think such a thing doesn't matter to me? When I have finished with him, he will wish that he had never been born! That I promise you, *yinéka*! He has me to reckon with now, not a woman who has no man to protect her!'

Charity trembled. She held his hand against her cheek, loving the feel of him. 'It wasn't like Faith. It wasn't! I know I shouldn't have gone out—' She raised her eyes to his. 'I should have sewn the button on your shirt and then none of this would have happened!'

The anger she expected never dawned. 'This is not a prison, Charity, that you can't go outside the front door—'

'But I was upset – and – and angry!'

He touched her hair, smoothing it away from her face. 'What was there to upset you? Because I wouldn't take you to the Acropolis this morning?'

She was shocked that he should think her so unreasonable. 'Oh, Loukos, no!' she protested. 'Only I saw you with Ariadne—' She blinked, sure now that he would turn away from her, but his smile held only an amused mockery that set her heart racing. She bit her lip. 'I'm sorry,' she said again.

'Ah yes, Ariadne,' he said thoughtfully. 'You should have more confidence in yourself, my ridiculous wife! But this is not the moment for long explanations about something which does not concern you. I have other things to do!' He bent his head and kissed her hard on the lips. 'No one takes liberties with my woman and gets away with it! He shall pay, and pay in full, for that!'

'Don't hurt him!' Charity begged.

Loukos frowned. 'Do you expect me to be gentle with such a man? I'd like to break his neck!'

'Yes, I know,' Charity said, surprised to discover that she did, and even more surprised to find that she could approve such an attitude. 'But Colin thinks you're terribly rich, and he'll sue you, and I couldn't bear that! That's why he wanted me and Alexander to go to England with him! He – he thinks Alexander inherited a whole lot of money from Nikos – *a million pounds*! – and that an English court would award me custody. So you see–'

'And what was he going to do about your marriage to me?'

Charity blushed. 'He talked about having it annulled. I told him that wasn't – wasn't possible, but he said you'd let me go soon enough when you discovered I was with him. I thought so too,' she added in an undertone.

Loukos gave her a brilliant look. 'That's something else that I intend to put right! Do exactly as my mother tells you and be good! I'll be back as soon as I can be, and I expect to find you looking a lot better than you do now!'

Charity felt quite dazed with happiness. She sat back against the cushions and watched him go, her mind leaping ahead to his return. She heard the door close behind him and smiled at her mother-in-law with a new confidence. Then another thought struck her and she started to her feet.

'He doesn't know where Colin is!' she exclaimed.

Xenia smiled a small, enigmatic smile; the smile that the Greeks have always been famous for. 'He will find him,' she said.

Xenia suggested that Charity should rest in her room, but she didn't want to lie alone on the bed she had shared with Loukos.

'You have no need to worry, my daughter, he will exact a just revenge for the hurt that has been done to you,' her mother-in-law said in her awkward, slow English.

'But Colin might hurt him!'

Xenia dismissed that with the contempt it deserved.

'Loukos is a man, my dear. This Colin of yours is only greedy boy. How can he hurt Loukos?'

Charity acknowledged the justice of this. She knew that i was Colin she ought to be worrying about, but she was to tired to do more than hope that Loukos wouldn't actuall break his neck. How bloodthirsty she was becoming, sh rebuked herself, with such Greek ideas about vengeance She was not at all the civilized young woman she ha thought herself to be! She looked up and met Xenia' amused eyes.

'Will Loukos hurt him?' she asked.

Xenia patted her arm. 'Of course. He will find a way. Di you think your husband would do less when another man ha done this to you?'

Charity tried not to be pleased by the thought. 'I suppos it wouldn't matter if he'd bruised me and torn my clothe himself?'

Xenia accepted this without batting an eye. 'He is you husband,' she said indifferently. 'You look exhausted, m dear. Why don't you rest awhile? Or at least change you clothes and wash your poor face? Electra will make yo something to eat, and I will put some ointment on th scratches on your legs. Yes?'

Charity rose reluctantly to her feet, pulling a face whe she looked down and saw the sad state of her stockings. 'I' not very hungry,' she said. 'My head aches and I'm stiff!'

'A hot bath will revive you,' Xenia insisted. She waite until Charity was almost at the door and then lifted a com manding hand. 'By the way,' she said, her eyes on the sewin on her knee, 'Ariadne is to be married to some man in Cor inth. Go and have your bath, my dear, and Electra will tal to you while you eat. She finds it easier to speak in Englis than I. Our conversations will have to wait until you spea my language!'

And that would be a long time hence, Charity thought t herself, mildly irritated because she was beginning to thin that Xenia's English was quite as good as her sister's and only needed a little practice to perfect it, whereas her Greek was non-existent. Why, if she couldn't even get a taxi-driver to understand a simple address, what on earth could make her mother-in-law imagine that they would ever be able to hold cosy conversations together in that language?

The hot water was comforting to her ill-used body after all and she felt considerably better by the time she had bathed and changed. Even her head had stopped aching unless she was jolted, or bent down to pick up something off the floor. She was hungry too, despite her earlier denials. She went into the kitchen with a shamed expression on her face, and smiled at Electra who was giving Alexander the last of his bottle.

On the table was Loukos' shirt, the missing button neatly replaced. Charity fingered the collar thoughtfully. 'You should have left it for me to do,' she said. 'It's my job now.' She thought how she had thrown the shirt on the floor and coloured a little. 'I would have done it in the end!'

'You did the washing,' Electra answered.

Yes, Charity thought, she had done the washing! And if she knew anything about it, she had done it so badly that Electra had probably had to do it all over again.

Electra finished feeding Alexander and murmured to him in Greek as she got awkwardly to her feet. 'Will you put him in his cot while I heat you some soup?' she asked Charity.

Charity accepted the task with alacrity. 'If I didn't care for myself, I should have thought about him before charging out of here this morning. Colin doesn't see him as a person at all. He doesn't *care*—'

'Now, now, stop your fretting,' Electra advised. 'You brought him back safe enough!'

Charity hesitated. 'Did Nikos leave Alexander a lot of money?' she asked bluntly.

Electra's dark eyes flew to her face. 'What if he did?'

'I thought he and Faith didn't have any money. The

house they were living in at Arachova looked so dreadfull poor!'

'Iphigenia's house? Iphigenia has no money. Wher would she get money from? She has been a widow ever sinc her husband was killed in the war. It has not been easy fo her. It has not been easy for any of us who were left alon even those of us who had our families to support us.'

Charity was startled. 'But I thought Faith had been livin there?'

'Iphigenia's is a clean house!'

'Yes, I know. I'm not being critical, only I can't thin where they all slept – and if Nikos had so much money surely they could have found somewhere a little mor comfortable?'

'They went first to a hotel,' Electra explained grimly, 'bu your sister didn't like to live in public in her condition Nikos was naturally welcome in every house in both Delph and Arachova and he was out a great deal. Faith would no learn to speak Greek, so there was no point in her visitin with the other women as she would have been welcome t do. She wanted Nikos with her morning, noon and night, bu Nikos was not that kind of a man. She thought, no doubt, they had a house he would stay in with her more. Iphigeni was in need of the money and so she agreed for them to hav her house, while she went to live with her daughter furthe down the hill. But Nikos saw no reason to spend his even ings at home even then.'

'I think that was mean!' Charity burst out.

Electra shrugged. 'He came home in the end. It was fo Faith to learn Greek and to interest herself in the women' affairs in the village.'

'Perhaps she didn't feel able to while she was pregnant Charity defended her dead sister. 'Some women don't wan to do anything at that time.'

'Perhaps.' Electra poured the hot soup into a bowl 'Perhaps not.'

'You still blame her, don't you?'

Electra put the saucepan in the sink, turning her back on Charity and making a great noise with the water as she poured it into the dirty pan. 'None of us can know what happened at the last. Perhaps she had reason to behave as she did and go rushing off to Athens, sending for you, and planning to run away from her husband. But most of her troubles were of her own making. She made it impossible for us to help her, and impossible for us to defend her against others too. She would not make allowances for our customs, and that angered many of our friends. We may be Greek and old-fashioned in our ways, but we are not always wrong!'

'But, if Nikos had so much money—'

Electra cut up some bread and put it on the tray beside the bowl of soup. 'When he left the company, Loukos forbade him to use any of the shares he held in the shipping line. Producing plays at Delphi couldn't go on for ever, and then what was he going to do? He would have a wife and child to support and he had to remember that. He would have gone back to the family business in the end.'

Charity transferred Alexander from one arm to the other. 'Did Faith know that?' she asked.

Electra came over to her and whisked the baby away from her. 'Faith? Why should she know anything about it? It was between Loukos and Nikos!' She laughed harshly and carried Alexander away to his cot without a backward look.

Charity carried her tray into the living-room, avoiding her mother-in-law's inquiring glance as to what she and Electra had been talking about. 'Do you think Loukos will be long?' she asked involuntarily.

Xenia merely went on with her sewing. Charity drank her soup, amusing herself by tearing up the bread into pieces and dunking it into the liquid. 'I don't think it's much fun being a woman, if all one has to do is sit around and wait all the time!' she went on. 'How you keep so calm when – when *anything* might be happening, I don't know!'

173

Xenia smiled. 'Loukos said you were to rest—'

'No, he didn't! He said he expected me to be looking better, which isn't the same thing at all!'

'And are you feeling better?'

Charity nodded, a little ashamed of her outburst. She sighed. 'Do you think he will be long?'

'You have already asked me that,' her mother-in-law returned with a smile. 'I think he will be too long for me to have to watch you prowling about like a – what is the word? – like a *tigger*. You should have a hobby to keep you occupied when these things happen.'

Charity burst into delighted laughter. 'I hope they won't happen very often!' She broke off, suddenly nervous again. 'Supposing – supposing something has happened to him! I'd never forgive myself! I wish he'd taken me with him!'

'That would have been quite unsuitable!' Xenia glanced across at her. 'Is there nothing you can do to amuse yourself? What do you do to amuse yourself when you are at home in England?'

'I don't know,' Charity admitted. 'I walk, and I like looking at places, things like that.'

Xenia gave her a brilliant smile, so like her son's that Charity felt quite bemused. 'Then go now and look at the Acropolis! We shall be very happy not to have you here looking like a ghost, and starting at every sound in case it is Loukos! Go out and enjoy yourself, my dear!'

Charity was tempted. 'But Loukos will come back here,' she objected.

'Electra and I will be here. We will send him to find you the moment he returns.' She gave her daughter-in-law an ironic look. 'There will be no family there to witness what he says to you. Sometimes it is good for a man and his wife to speak alone, no?'

'You're a darling!' Charity said warmly. She flung her arms around Xenia's dumpy form and kissed her cheek. 'But you will tell Loukos it was your idea, won't you?' She grinned. 'He did say that I was to do everything you told me to!'

Xenia repaired her ruffled dignity with a faint smile. 'I will explain to him *exactly*,' she promised. 'Now, please go before I stick this needle into myself, or do one of us a worse injury!'

Charity chuckled. 'I'm already gone!' she claimed, and she rushed down the corridor to collect her coat.

CHAPTER TWELVE

THEY told her the Acropolis was due to close at sunset. It was already half past four, so that gave her, at most, just over half an hour in which to make her first pilgrimage to the Athenian citadel of the gods, the high place of the city, where the ancient Greeks had always placed their temples and religious buildings. Charity refused to consider that she might have to leave before Loukos came to join her there. It was, though she didn't know why, terribly important to her that he should come to her there, where the heroes of Athens had always come.

She stood at the foot of the southern slope looking upwards and wondered at her own callousness that could allow her to enjoy such a sight while her husband was out exacting revenge on her behalf from a man she had always liked until that day. Yet, if she felt anything, it was not compassion for Colin, it was a fierce pride that because she was Loukos' wife he would allow no harm to come to her from anyone else without paying a heavy penalty for daring to touch her. It was a rough kind of loving, but it was all she had.

The zig-zag path led upwards to the Propylaea, the magnificent entrance to the Acropolis, over rough slabs of marble that must have once made sense, but now lay, higgledy-piggledy, making one watch one's footsteps as one climbed steadily to the top. For more than the first two thousand years of its existence, the Propylaea had remained remarkably intact. The Turks had used it as a munitions store, and unfortunately some of the munitions had blown up, taking the roof and some of the supporting walls with it. Some very good restoration had been done to show what it must have been like, though, and Charity had no difficulty in imagining what it had been like in the days of Pericles, when it had just been built, and a stream of worshippers had come and gone through its portals, some of them leading the animals doomed to be sacrificed, their feet slithering on the grooved marble pavements.

She thought she would get the best view of the city beneath her from the Temple of the Wingless Victory and wandered across the rough ground to the platform where the comparatively small temple stood. In the days when the gods had walked the earth, both Poseidon, the god of the sea, and Athene, the goddess of wisdom, had wanted Athens for their own. Poseidon had beaten the ground with his trident, giving Athens her access to the sea. Athene had offered the people the olive tree, which was sacred to her cult, and had gained their allegiance to her cause and had given her name to the city which was now considered hers. So the temple had once housed her statue, holding the owl, the symbol of wisdom, in one hand, and the Victory in the other. Most Victories were depicted with wings on their backs, but this one had been carved out of olive wood and had had no wings. It was said that the Athenians had clipped its wings to make sure it stayed amongst them. It had been lost a long, long time ago, but the temple remained, its perfect proportions visible for miles across the city.

Charity had hoped to see the eastern side of the Parthenon and the frieze which depicted Apollo, just as she had seen it on the cover of the book. There was very little left of the eastern wall, however. She could see, across the way, the hill from which the Venetians had blasted the building during their seige of the city two or three hundred years ago, with a total disregard for the historical value of the site that had been characteristic of their age.

It was harder to imagine what the Parthenon had been like in the full flush of its prime. Now only the skeleton was left, with none of the gold and scarlet and black that had once covered the exterior. Charity had been told that the

Parthenon represented Athene in her masculine guise, dressed in armour, and ready to defend her city; the third temple, the Erechtheum, had held her statue dressed in a more feminine guise, a gentleness which lingers on in the six statues of the famous Caryatids, the dancing maidens, one of which was taken away by Lord Elgin to the British Museum, causing such distress amongst her sisters that they are said to have moaned in sympathy all through the night. She has been replaced by a cast made from the original, but the substitute is cracking under the strain and is easy to pick out from the others.

Charity spent a long time looking at the Parthenon. It pleased her that no two pillars were quite the same and that the spaces between them varied enormously, and yet, taken as a whole, the proportions looked exactly right and were far more satisfying then any mathematical design.

It was in the museum that Charity discovered the statue of Apollo she had wanted to see. He sat at his ease between Poseidon and Artemis, his head turned towards the sea-god as if they were having a friendly conversation. Close to, the resemblance to Loukos was astonishing. Perhaps Apollo's face was softer and his chin less firm, but that might have been no more than the weathering of centuries. The likeness was sufficiently strong to bring the tears starting to Charity's eyes and her heart dissolved within her at the sight of him. Would he never come?

She stood in front of the remnant of the frieze, wishing that she could touch the marble face in front of her, but sure that such an action would not be popular with the custodian who was standing not far away from her. She thought of the coin and the piece of laurel that she left as an offering for Apollo at his shrine in Delphi.

'You failed me,' she told him.

Apollo went on with his conversation with Poseidon, ignoring the female who stood before him. What had Pericles said of the women of ancient Athens? That a virtuous woman was one about whom nothing was said, either to her praise or blame, or words to that effect? Athenian women had been married for their fortunes, had been kept closely confined to their homes, and had provided their husbands with their legitimate children. When their men had wanted female companionship, they had gone elsewhere, to the women of other cities, who might have been less respectable, but who seemed to have a great deal more fun.

Like Ariadne!

'You failed me,' Charity said again. 'I only wanted to be myself. Was that so much to ask?'

Yet Ariadne was to marry a man from Corinth, if Xenia could be believed.

'I wanted to be someone, but I couldn't even be that, because Loukos must have loved her – and he can't love both of us, can he?'

Apollo, frozen in stone, continued to ignore her complaint. He was not really like Loukos at all. Loukos had never turned away from her distress, not even when he had first met her at the Tower of the Winds.

They were starting to shut up the little museum and she turned away from the frieze and went back outside, hoping to see the sun set behind the Erechtheum before she had to go down from the Acropolis. If Loukos was coming, he would have to come soon, she thought. Her longing for him settled like a pain within her as the wind caught and buffeted her in the open space between the two temples.

When she looked down the western side of the Acropolis, she found herself searching automatically for the Tower of the Winds, and knew it was because she connected it with Loukos; that whenever she saw him she would live again that moment when he had come striding towards her, looking like Apollo come to life. She went round the side of the temple, standing right on the edge of the steep slope that fell to the street below. She put her hand on the Pentelic marble of the temple and climbed up higher still into a perch that had been torn from a fallen column. The sun was casting a reddish glow across the whole western sky. It was strangely beautiful, and made more so by some threatening thunder clouds that were coming up from the north. Beyond the horizon, the lightning flashed, but there was no immediate danger from the rain.

Down there somewhere was an ancient temple that had been converted into a Christian church. It had become known to the local people as St George the Lazy, because they had blamed the saint and not the Turkish overlords for the scarcity of the masses that had been celebrated there. Charity smiled at the thought, but she could not stop herself from thinking of what Loukos was doing for all this time, and the smile died.

Where was Loukos? She had only a few more minutes and then she would have to go. She shut her eyes and thought about the way Colin had dismissed her marriage as if it were a thing of no account. She owed him one for that, she thought, for it was infinitely precious to her. Yet, in a strange way, she was grateful to him too, for he had made her burningly aware of her pride in being Loukos' wife, and no one could take that away from her.

She stretched upwards and took a deep breath, filling her lungs with the golden evening air.

'*I am Mrs. Loukos Papandreous!*' she announced in a loud voice. It seemed she was someone after all.

She was lifted down from her perch by a pair of strong hands she would have known anywhere. 'Loukos!' she exclaimed, her face alight with pleasure. 'You did come!'

He smiled. 'So Apollo worked a small miracle for you after all,' he said.

She shook her head, her eyes shy. 'No, not Apollo,' she denied. 'You did.'

He gave her a curious glance. 'Have you sorted us out in your mind at last?' he inquired, his voice very gentle.

'I think so. I know now who I want to be. I want to be

your wife, Loukos. On any terms, I want to be your wife!'

He pulled her against him, touching the bruise on the side of her head. '*Agapi mou*, I never doubted it. Do you think that I don't know that you love me? After last night, how could I not have known?'

Charity flushed, and changed the subject. 'Did you find Colin?'

'I did.'

The grimness of his tone frightened her. 'Loukos, you didn't hurt him, did you?'

'I did what had to be done.'

'But you don't know Colin! It wasn't wise to make an enemy of him. If he can get back at you he will, and I couldn't bear that!'

'Colin and I understand each other very well. There is no need for you to worry yourself about him.' He smiled down at her. 'Women complicate such matters and are far better kept out when men come to an agreement—'

'You can't persuade me that Colin agreed to anything!'

'Why not?'

'D-did he? I thought perhaps you would hit him, and – and he wouldn't be likely to forgive that!'

Loukos laughed. 'And you were pleased that I should do such a thing for you? Do you now wish to hear all the details so that you can gloat over his downfall?'

'Not really,' she said. 'Though I haven't nearly such a nice nature as I thought. Loukos, did you hit him?'

'I did.'

Her eyes widened. 'But you didn't hurt him? Not *really* hurt him?'

He touched the bruise on her head again, his lips tightening. 'He has a black eye and a bruise to match yours—'

'And he didn't even *touch* you!' Charity exclaimed, much gratified.

'Nor will he touch you again!' His hands pressed her closer to him with a strength that would not be denied, just as the sun descended beyond the horizon, a great swollen, scarlet ball that sent thick fingers of colour running up the sky towards the coming storm clouds.

'It was partly my fault,' Charity confessed. 'I never should have asked him to come here in the first place, but he was the only man I knew, and I thought if I were to get married you'd let me have Alexander as my sister wanted. I thought I knew everything there was to know about him, but I didn't know him at all.' She tilted her face impulsively the better to see her husband. 'Was Nikos really a rich man?' she asked him. 'Did he leave it all to Alexander?'

Loukos looked amused. 'Didn't you know? I thought sometimes that you didn't, but I couldn't imagine Faith having kept quiet about such a thing. Did she never write and tell you of the rich man she had married?'

Charity shook her head, remembering how the lack of letters had hurt her. 'I told you she wasn't a good correspondent. A few postcards, that was all.' She pulled herself free of his restraining embrace. 'You think that's why I came here in the first place, don't you?' She was a good deal upset and her head was beginning to ache again. 'I thought you at least liked me, but I don't see how you can when you don't even trust me! I didn't know! I didn't!'

'What I think doesn't matter,' he answered. 'I had to protect Alexandros, whatever I thought.'

She felt completely beaten. 'We ought to be going,' she said.

He sighed, looking at her white, miserable face. 'If I thought it, I had no reason to expect anything else, from what Faith had told us about her family. All we knew was that none of you came to see her—'

'She never asked us to!'

'I know that now. I have learned much about you, my Charity, but *then*, when all I knew was that I wanted to kiss you and make love to you, and have you look at me with those wide eyes of yours as though I were indeed a god come to court you, I only knew that you were Faith's sister and that she had married Nikos for his money, though she came to love him in time.'

'I didn't know!' Charity breathed.

'About your sister?' His brilliant eyes burned into hers, making her forget all about her brief anger with him.

'What you wanted!'

'To make love to you? My foolish Charity, I think you might have learned something about me last night too – if you had had your wits about you!' He reached down and kissed her and she could feel his laughter against her lips. 'I see I shall have to do better tonight! Will you like that? Will you welcome me as ardently as you did—?'

She cut him off with a quick kiss, hotly embarrassed by his words, dodging away from him, and averting her face from his observant eyes to hide her blushes.

'What did you do with Colin?' she asked.

He laughed out loud. 'I think that might have told you something too!' he mocked her, enjoying her discomfiture. 'Colin is waiting for his aeroplane at the airport. A policeman and I saw him personally through the passport control. Technically, he has already left Greece, but just in case there is someone watching him to make sure he does not come back!' He stopped laughing. '*I* do not pretend that it is small-minded to be jealous, Charity. Have I any reason to be jealous of Colin Anderson? Did you ever feel for him more than a young girl feels for any man who notices her, when she is still unsure of what it means to be a woman?'

Charity stared at him, silently shaking her head. 'Are you jealous of *me*?' she asked.

'You are my woman,' he said roughly. 'Isn't that enough for you?'

'Yes, of course it is.' But she wished he would speak of loving her as well. She turned her head to see the last of the sunset, shaken by the strength of the longing within her. 'We must go down,' she said aloud. 'They told me they closed at sunset.'

They walked down the zig-zag path together, hand in hand. She had so much, Charity told herself, she was being greedy to want him to put his love into words, especially if he didn't love her. At least he wanted her and liked to make love to her, and, when Ariadne was safely married, perhaps he would forget his earlier love and come to love her too in every way, just as she loved him. She would wait willingly for that day if it took half her life and, in the meantime, she would have more of him than any other woman would ever have – even Ariadne!

'Are we going home?' she asked him as they reached the foot of the hill, where there are some souvenir stalls, and where the sponge-sellers stand in the daytime.

'Not yet, my dear. We have some more talking to do before we go home. There are some questions I want to ask you–' he smiled at her nervous start – 'and something I wish to tell you as well.'

She searched her mind for what he might want to ask her, a puzzled look on her face. 'We could walk home,' she suggested.

'Oh no, you don't escape as easily as that!' he retorted. 'We will go over to that restaurant over there and order some tea. We will go home only after we have finished our talk. My mother and Electra will be waiting for us at home! There is always somebody else there, and for a little while, I want you all to myself!' He smiled, his eyes more brilliant than ever. 'My mother was very concerned for you, did you know that? She seemed to think that you are afraid of me. Are you, Charity?'

'Not afraid,' she said quickly. 'A little nervous of you, perhaps.'

'Because I am Greek and a foreigner to you?'

'N-no,' she stammered. 'I don't know what you expect from me–'

He frowned. 'I thought I'd made that quite clear!' he

184

teased her, but he wasn't laughing at her as she had been afraid he would. 'Perhaps I expect too much of an Englishwoman who considers herself the equal of any man?'

She tried to laugh with him, but failed miserably. 'I d-don't consider myself your equal,' she managed, setting off down the cobbled road at a great pace.

'Oh?' He sounded so interested that her spirits failed her. 'Tell me more!'

'It's – it's obvious!'

'To me? Or to you?'

She swallowed. 'To me. You're – you're physically stronger, and you're richer than I am, and – and you expect me to obey you. You *told* me so! And anyway, I – I like it that way!'

He was silent. She cast him a quick glance, wishing that she had held her tongue. The traffic swished past them, holding them prisoner on the edge of the pavement. Loukos put his hand under her elbow and guided her across the busy street at the first opportunity, leading the way through the gate and into the restaurant beyond. The tables were covered with colourful cloths that were matched by the napkins and the bright vases of flowers. A few students were seated at one of the tables, arguing amiably over steaming mugs of hot chocolate. Otherwise the place was deserted.

'If we sit over there, we can talk without being disturbed,' Loukos suggested, pointing to a table in the far corner. He sat down on the inside seat, so that he could look not only at her but all that was happening behind her, while she, perforce, had only him to look at.

'I don't see that there's anything to talk about!' she declared belligerently, afraid of what else he would make her say in an unguarded moment. That was the trouble, she thought. He knew a great deal too much about her, while he remained as mysterious as ever, and it was all the fault of her stupid tongue! There had been no reason to tell him anything at all!

185

He lifted his eyebrows in open mockery, but his expression was very gentle. 'What will you have?' he asked her. 'Tea? Cakes?'

Charity nodded. She didn't care what she ate. 'What questions do you want to ask me?' she burst out.

'I want to know what it was that upset you this morning.'

She blinked. Her mouth felt dry and her tongue at least two sizes too large for her mouth. 'It was silly—' She waited for him to say something, but he went on sitting there, patiently waiting for her to continue. 'You said you had to work!' She cast him an indignant look, but she couldn't keep it up. She didn't feel angry any more. What had she to be indignant about? He had never pretended to her that he loved her. 'I wouldn't have minded if it had been anywhere else, or – or another time! Did you have to kiss Ariadne *there*, and so soon *after last night*?'

'Are you going to be small-minded enough to be jealous after all?'

'*No!*' she denied hotly. 'I knew all about Ariadne. But I thought—'

'Who told you about Ariadne?' he asked severely.

She bent her head. 'Electra,' she murmured.

'I think you'd better tell me what she told you,' he insisted. 'I thought we'd managed to keep the whole story away from the family.'

'Families always know that sort of thing!' Charity declared, feeling a little more brave. 'There's always someone to tell them about it!'

He grinned, amused. 'I daresay you're right,' he agreed. 'Well, Charity?'

'She said that Ariadne was your mistress and that you were very much in love with her, but that you wouldn't marry her because—' she coloured fiercely – 'because Greek men don't!' she went on desperately. 'Though if you love someone, really love someone, I don't see why not!' she

186

added.

She found his amusement very disturbing to her composure. 'It's because of an old belief,' he said, 'that if a woman will give herself to a man once without marriage, she may very well do so again. It is not a trait we welcome in our wives!'

'Oh,' said Charity.

'What else did Electra tell you?'

'She said that Ariadne's family were hardly speaking to her. You're not a very forgiving people, are you?'

Loukos shook his head. 'Our hatreds are as old as Homer, that's why we make such good lovers!' His eyes glimmered with laughter. 'Did you believe Electra?' he asked suddenly.

'Of course,' she said. 'I'd seen you together, after all.'

'Then why did you agree to marry me?'

Her breath caught in the back of her throat. 'You know why!' Charity bit her lip, not looking at him. 'Your mother says Ariadne is to marry some man from Corinth.'

'Nauplia,' he corrected. 'I suppose she thinks she knows all about it too.' He reached across the table and took Charity's hand in his own, making sure that he had her full attention. 'I'm beginning to understand why you thought my Ariadne, as you called her, had fallen for the wrong god. But I was never in love with her, nor she with me. I wasn't going to tell you. It has caused enough trouble, and why should you be burdened with the knowledge of something that is none of your business?'

'You don't have to tell me,' she said uncomfortably.

'No?' His expression softened and she caught a glimpse of something in his eyes that set her heart racing. 'I think we owe you the whole story, my love, if the mere sight of Ariadne's kiss of gratitude for sorting out her life can upset you enough—'

'It didn't look like gratitude!' she interrupted tartly.

He shrugged. 'Ariadne is an actress. She makes the most

of any scene. You may believe me that it was only gratitude, though, because she has never liked me very much, not even now I have found her a husband and provided her with a substantial enough dowry to make him marry her! It was always Nikos with her. When he married Faith, she became engaged to another man and we all hoped for the best. But it was not to be. Nikos asked her to go to Delphi, to be with him, and they had a rather unsatisfactory affair. I think Nikos was tired of being nagged by your sister, and Ariadne never made that mistake! When Faith found out, as she was bound to do, she determined to leave Nikos and take the baby with her. That is when she sent for you.'

The colour drained from Charity's face. 'But you all said that *she* was to blame!'

'Your sister was very much at fault! She made no secret of why she had married Nikos. If he had been a poor man, he would never have had a chance with her! When he decided to go to Delphi, she fought him all the way and made his life a misery because there was no doubt about how he felt about her. As his wife, she should have foreseen that he would find comfort somewhere else. She should have changed her ways and made him want to come back to her, especially when she found that she needed him and, maybe, even loved him herself. She should have waited in his house with her son and learned what it means to be a wife instead of a spoilt child! But she was too angry to think of anyone but herself. First, she sends for you whom she has not seen or bothered about for years! Then she flings herself out of the house when Nikos tries to have things out with her, killing both herself and him. Neither of them had any business to be driving in such an emotional atmosphere, and all of it quite unnecessary!'

To Charity it sounded a harsh judgment on her impetuous, self-absorbed sister. No, the Greeks did not forgive easily, she thought with a shiver. They had found Faith wanting in the womanly qualities they held to be so important and they had condemned her for not being like them-selves. But it had not been all her fault.

'She probably didn't know what to do,' Charity excused her. 'I can understand how she felt.'

'I wouldn't allow you to leave me under any circum-stances!' he bit out with superb arrogance. He sounded very sure of himself. But then, Charity reflected, he had reason to be. She had told him that she wanted to be his wife on any terms, and she had proved it by marrying him when she had thought him in love with Ariadne.

She smiled. 'How would you stop me?'

'I'd find a way. I don't think your defences would be very strong against me if I made up my kind to turn you into a loving wife. Your red hair doesn't only make you bad-tem-pered!' His eyes laughed into hers. 'Besides,' he added, 'your warm heart would betray you. You would worry about me and you'd have to come back to see if I was perfectly happy without you, feeling as guilty as if you'd murdered me!'

'I would not!' The remarkable lack of conviction in her denial made her want to laugh. How ridiculous she was being, when they both knew that nothing would make her leave him, no matter what he did to her. 'Poor Faith!' she sighed. 'I wish she'd been happier.'

Loukos' eyes met hers and she thought she caught a flicker of anxiety in his. 'Are you happy, loving me?' he asked.

'Very happy,' she responded. There would be times, she knew, when she would long for the land where she had been born and had grown up, when she would long even more for the sound of her own language and the different customs of her English friends, but there would never be a time when she would regret being Loukos' wife. She gave him a brief look of inquiry. 'What was it you were going to tell me? Or was it that, about Faith?'

He shook his head. 'It's something I should have told you long ago, but I thought you already knew.' He fingered the ring on her hand with a slight smile. 'My darling Charity, didn't you really guess that I love you? That I determined to marry you and make you mine when I first saw you at the Tower of the Winds? But what must you do but produce this Colin of yours whom anyone could see would never appreciate you or make you happy! Didn't you feel that I loved you when I kissed you on Christmas Day, or at Daphni when you would only promise to marry me because I could offer you Alexandros?'

She gazed at him, wide-eyed. 'I only knew that I had fallen fathoms deep in love with you,' she confessed. 'I didn't know what to do!'

'And last night? You must have known that I loved you!'

'You never said so,' she said in a low voice. 'I thought that you were content that I loved you. And I do, Loukos. I love you so much that it hurts! You don't know how much! I don't expect you to love me like that, but if you could love me a little bit—' She broke off at the look on his face. 'Loukos?'

'A little bit!' he repeated. 'I spent most of the night telling you how much I loved you! Oh, Charity, *agapi mou*, my darling, the sooner you learn some Greek the better!' A muscle flickered in his cheek. 'Though you must have a very odd idea of me if you think I could make love to anyone who was not my beloved as I made love to you last night!'

'I thought—' she began. She veiled her eyes with her eyelashes, peeping at him through them, delighted to find that she had the power to move him, just as he could make her melt inside with love for him. 'You may not be Apollo,' she went on, smiling a little, 'but, to me, you are one of the godlike kind of men. You had only to look at me and what chance did a mere mortal like me have?'

He caressed the back of her neck with a fierce possessiveness that made her gasp. 'None at all!' he said. 'Let's go home, Charity. We'll send Alexandros and Electra to stay with my mother for a while. I find I want to have my wife to myself for a bit.'

She looked up. 'Loukos, you do *indeed* love me?'

'I do indeed love you,' he agreed, smiling at her earnestness. 'And, quite shortly, I shall prove it to you all over again!'